Francis Louis Guy Smith

Donagon

ISBN:1500821098
ISBN-13:9781500821098

Published by Books by Guy Inc.
Salado, Texas

Dedication

To all the women of the west who had to endure hardships and especially those who were held captive by the hostile nations of a people who were being invaded.

Acknowledgments

For all scripture verses, The New American Standard version of the Holy Bible. I don't think the Lord will mind. For all historical locales and characters, Wikipedia, the free on line encyclopedia.

Foreword

Many of us find it hard to imagine the hardships faced by Texans in the early eighteen hundreds. Francis Louis Guy Smith tells the story of an orphaned boy as he struggles into manhood with obstacles at every turn. This story of friendship, loyalty, and determination, he has written without compromising Christian values for story enhancement. A great read!

Dennis Johnson.... Retired Texas Parks and Wildlife.

Chapter 1

Pure and undefiled religion in the sight of our God and Father
is this: to visit orphans and widows in their distress, and to keep
oneself unstained by the world. James 1:27

San Antonio, Texas in the year eighteen thirty six
was a mission under attack by General Antonio Lopez
de Santa Anna. Donald Arturo Donagon was on the
side of the Texas revolution. He had gone to Gonzales
to help Sam Houston in the battle for Texas
Independence.

That left Maria, his wife of thirteen years, alone in San Antonio to take care of their twelve-year-old son, David.

When Donald Donagon was in the number of men assassinated by the army of Santa Anna at Goliad, there was no one to support his wife and son. Maria had no one to turn to, since she had married against her father's wishes.

Her family had come from Germany when she was only a baby, and her father held his family to the strict standards of the church.

Girls of the German, Jewish faith were to marry only men of their own faith. Maria, had been swept off her feet, by Donald Arturo Donagon and gone against her family's orders.

She was no longer welcome in their home.

Having no one to turn to after her husband's death, she had to work the cantinas and saloons to find food for her and her son. There were times when she scoured the alleys and trashcans from general stores and cafés just to survive.

It was in one of those alleys that David Donagon found his mother. A drunken soldier had beaten her to death. Now, the twelve year old was all alone in a world with nowhere to turn.

He had made friends with two other boy's whose fathers and mothers had met the same fate as his own. Their mothers, left widows of the war, had few choices but to turn to a life of sinful acts.

Marcus 'Bud' Maxwell and Jason 'Little Henry' Jones made up a trio of young boys with no way to survive, but by stealing from drunk soldiers and others who they found lying in alleys and livery stables.

One of those who they attempted to rob, was not as drunk as they thought. He pulled a six-gun and marched the three boys down the main street of San Antonio to the sheriff's office.

The sheriff locked the three orphans in a cell with two other men who he arrested for firing their weapons into the air. They were cowhands from a herd on the edge of town.

At first light, another man came to bail the two men out of jail because he needed them to help drive a herd of longhorns from San Antonio to New Orleans.

"Sheriff, what you got these other three locked up for?"

"They was trying to rob a man in an alley. Probably looking for something to eat. Bunch of younguns around town like them. Pa's got killed in the war and no telling where their Ma's are."

"How much is their bail?"

"Ain't no bail. Can't keep em. You need em, go ahead and take em. Might straighten em out to go where you going."

"You boys want to go on a trail drive to New Orleans?"

"Where's New Orleans?" Bud asked.

"What's a trail drive?" Little Henry chimed in.

"You boys own a horse?"

"No sir."

"You know how to ride a horse?"

"Yessir."

They all three answered. All were lying. None of them had ever been in a saddle.

"Let em out sheriff. We'll see what they can do." The man who got them out of jail turned and walked away.

When they were out on the street, David Donagon turned to the man.

"Mister, do we get paid to do this?"

"Thirty a month and found. Get paid when the drive is done."

Neither of them had ever seen thirty dollars at one time. When the man walked down the street, Bud turned to his two friends. "What's found?"

The other two shrugged their shoulders.

"Herd is on the north side of town, by the river. We leave at first light! Be there!"

"Mister, you got a name?" Donagon asked.

"I'm Alphonse P. Boudreau."

"Mister, do we have to wait to morning. Can we go with you now? We might not be able to find you tomorrow. Do we get to eat on this trail drive?" Little Henry could hear his stomach growling.

"Come ahead. We'll find you something to eat. You going to earn every bite!"

——————— ….. ———————

For the first time since their fathers had gone away, someone handed the three boys tin plates with large steaks and beans piled high.

"Mister, if I eat this, can I have another one?" Little Henry was already looking for his second helping.

"Name is Stepwilder. John J. Stepwilder. I ain't no nurse maid, boy. You just worry about what you got. If'n you still hongry, I'll see can I find another one. Best eat that and go to sleep. Five o'clock gonna

9

come early. You boys got to get them steers started to New Awlins."

"What did he say?" Bud looked at the others.

"He said, shut up and eat!"

Before first light, the man who had given them the steaks began banging on a triangle and yelling at them.

"Daylights a burning. Roll it out boys. Coffee's hot. Beans and biscuits over the fire. Let's go. Mister Boudreau ain't gonna wait all day!"

Boudreau was standing by a wagon with a cup of coffee in his hand.

"You boys know anything about wrangling horses?"

By the look on their faces, he knew the answer.

"You'll learn. Hey, Rankin. Find these three a saddle and show em how to put them on a horse. Don't give em no rank ones. They still wet behind the ears. Ain't got over hugging on their momma's yet!"

"Mister! You don't talk about our mommas."

Donagon felt the hair bristle on his neck. All three of them still had fond memories of their mothers.

Boudreau saw the look in their eyes.

"Sorry boys. No harm meant." He remembered what the sheriff had said about their Ma.

After a few tries, they all three managed to get their mounts saddled and cinched tight. Reaching their left feet high for the stirrup, swung a leg over the saddle, and was sitting upright. For about five seconds. All three horses began to run and buck, and three new riders, hit the dust, headfirst.

"Get up and try that again, boys." Rankin shook his head.

It was another hour before the three new cowhands learned to lock their knees on the side of their horses and hold on. Finally, they were able to stay in the saddle and start the animals walking in a straight line.

Rankin explained to them what a wrangler did and they finally knew they were to drive the horses ahead of the cattle and provide mounts for all the drovers. At night, they picketed the horses and took turns spending the night with them. Their first day on the trail was a hard one. When the day was done, none could lift their leg over the saddle to dismount.

Boudreau saw their dilemma and rode to where Rankin was sitting horseback watching them. "Spect if you don't help them boys get down, they gonna have to sleep that way."

"I spect you right, Mister Boudreau, but I was so enjoying watching them try to dismount."

"We got cows to move, Mister Rankin. Best get em down."

"Yes sir." The top hand rode to their aid.

It took them more than an hour to picket the horses and make their way to the cook wagon. All three of them struggled to walk the short distance to the fire. Only the smell of coffee and beans got them there.

"You boys almost too late. Them waddies didn't leave you much." The cook was slapping a spoonful of beans on a plate. "Biscuits over yonder." He pointed to a box on the gate of the wagon. "You want coffee, it's in the pot. Ain't got time to wait on you babies."

"We ain't no babies!"

"What?"

"We ain't no babies! You take it back!" Bud Maxwell had had a long day, and his temper was flaring.

"Go sit down and eat yore beans youngster, fore you git yoreself hurt."

"You take it back!" Bud reached for a rifle that was propped against a wagon wheel.

"Look, boy." Stepwilder kicked the rifle from his hand before he could get a good grip. "You best go on about yore business. I ain't got time to fool with you."

"Come on, Bud. He ain't worth it." Little Henry touched his friend's arm. He and Donagon had seen his temper before. He had killed a man in a dark alley for calling him a baby. A life of scrounging the back alleys of San Antonio for food had hardened all three of them, but Bud Maxwell more than the other two.

———————— ….. ————————

It took more than a week on the trail to get their bodies used to sitting astride a horse all day. Bud was still angry at the cook, but the other two had talked him out of killing the man.

"You kill him, Bud, we won't have nothing to eat."

"I can cook!"

I don't think Mister Boudreau would keep you on if you did that. Best forget it" Donagon tried to calm his compadre.

Three weeks into the drive found them approaching the Sabine River that would take all day to cross. They had never seen a herd of cattle cross a river, and all three watched in awe at how the drovers got them into the water. Rankin had assigned two other drovers to help them get the remuda across the water. After they had gone ahead and staked the horses out, they rode back to the river to watch.

Boudreau saw them sitting on the Louisiana side of the river watching the crossing and rode to where they were.

"Who's watching the remuda?"

They looked at each other.

"Could be Indians about. Best get back to them horses."

"Indians!" Little Henry looked at the others with a surprised look on his face.

"Never know, around these parts. Keep on the lookout!" Boudreau rode off.

When they got back to the remuda, mosquitos were starting to bite. It was late in the day and the pesky little bugs were swarming all around their ears and eyes.

"I ain't never seen skeeters like this." Little Henry was constantly slapping at the side of his neck.

"You ain't seen nothing yet. Wait til we get in that big swamp!" One of the drovers spoke up.

Rankin rode up as they were talking about the pesky biters.

"Stepwilder will show you how to keep em off you. Cookie should be making something up right now. He'll show you when you get to the wagon."

The three boys hurriedly checked on the horses and rode to the cook wagon. John J. Stepwilder was mixing a potion of pine oil and beauty berry leaves.

"What's that?" Little Henry turned up his nose.

"Don't matter none to me, you don't want it! I reckon when you get enough of them skeeter bites, you'll be back."

Donagon and Bud began rubbing the smelly potion on their ears and neck.

"Look, Henry. It keeps them bugs off. Better get some, before it's all gone."

Henry held his hand out and Stepwilder poured the thick, oily liquid in it. Right away, the mosquitos stopped buzzing around his ears. He grinned. "Is it time to eat yet?"

Their first day in the land of the mosquito was long and hard. The herd was finally across and bedded down for the night. A bunch of worn out drovers came to sit quietly around a fire and eat their last meal of the day.

Tomorrow, they would start a trek across a wet, marshy land. Rankin quietly spoke to each man about nighthawk assignments.

Donagon would take the first watch on the remuda. No one had much to say. Most of the hands found their bedrolls and turned in for a well-deserved rest.

Chapter 2

For every beast of the forest is mine, The cattle on a
thousand hills. Psalm 50:10

It was not an easy ride across the flat land called
Louisiana. Alphonse Boudreau knew the lay of the
land, because he had crossed it before. Rankin had
been with him on one other drive. Both of them knew
the worst was yet to come.

Almost three weeks from the Sabine River crossing, they came upon a large body of water called the Atchafalaya Basin.

The boys driving the remuda were the first ones to see the tall cypress trees looming out of the murky water. Off to their right, Stepwilder drove the wagon near the bank of the basin and stopped.

Boudreau rode up to the point and stopped to take a long gander at the water level in the basin. He knew from that, he would have to take the herd on a northerly route around the swamp.

There were two ways to get around the huge body of swampy water. When it was low, the southern trail would be passable. There was no way he could make it this time. Heavy rains had raised the level to running over the bank.

Rankin rode alongside of the trail boss. "Looks like we get to take the long way."

"Looks that way. Oh, well. It'll only add another week. Turn em north."

Rankin rode to the point and told the riders to turn the herd north. The cook wagon and remuda had already settled in for the night.

"You ever seen anything like that before?" Little Henry looked at his two friends. "I don't like water. It was hard for me to cross that river back yonder. Hope we don't have to cross this."

In another two days, the herd found its way to one of the many way stations for cattle drives. Some enterprising businessmen, saw a need for resting places for cattle drives from Texas to New Orleans. They had built camps that almost resembled hotels in the middle of a low, swampy cattle trail. They knew that by now, the drovers would be tired and needing a drink and a real bed to sleep in.

"Look yonder. Somebody done built a big house out here in this swamp!"

Bud was the first one to spot the log building with smoke in the chimney.

Boudreau rode up. "We'll stay there tonight, boys. Find a spot on the other side of that building to stake the remuda. We'll have fresh food and whiskey tonight. All accept you three. You ain't old enough to drink." He rode away before they could respond.

They drew straws to see who would get first watch with the horses. Little Henry lost.

Donagon and Bud Maxwell threw a leg over and rode to where the smoke was billowing from a sod chimney. Boudreau and Rankin were already sitting at a long table in the large front room.

"Sit down, boys. Red beans and catfish coming right up."

"Catfish. I ain't never heard of no cat fish before. Do they meow like a cat?"

"No, son, but they will stick you with a spike, you ain't careful."

"I reckon I'll just eat me some of them beans." Bud didn't want no part of a fish that was part cat.

"Donagon looked at the plate of fish in front of Boudreau and Rankin. "I spect I'll try one of them fish."

They ate their fill and watched as the older men sipped on glasses filled to the brim with whiskey.

"Reckon one of you boys ought to go relieve your partner, so he can eat."

————— ….. —————

Bud got up, walked out on a big front porch, and gazed off toward the remuda. He could not see Little Henry, but there was a glow from a low fire where he ought to be. He stepped off the porch and walked toward the flames, using them to guide his way. When he got to the fire, he looked around for Little Henry, but saw him nowhere.

"Henry? Where are you, Henry?"

"Here. I'm over here." A voice came out of the darkness closer to the bank of the basin.

"What you doing out there?"

"I don't feel so good."

"What's wrong?"

"I don't know. I'm just hot all over. Feels like them skeeters bitin me all over. I got too hot by that fire, so I come over here by the water where it's cooler."

"Maybe you ought to go get something to eat. They got some kinda red bean, and a fish that meows like a cat. I didn't eat any of that!"

"I don't want nothing to eat. Just need some cold water."

Bud got a canteen and held it out to his friend. The heat from his hand as he reached for it was hot enough for him to feel without even touching Little Henry.

"You are hot. I better go get Stepwilder. He'll know what to do." Before Henry could answer, Bud had stood and walked away.

Bud saw Donagon coming his way before he got to the building.

"Little Henry's sick. He's hotter'n a poker. We better get Stepwilder."

Both boys turned and returned to the building where Stepwilder was drinking with Boudreau and Rankin.

"Mister Stepwilder, Little Henry's sick. Bud said he's burning up."

The three men looked at one another.

"We better go see. He might have the fever." Boudreau got to his feet, followed by Rankin and Stepwilder.

By the time they reached the boy, he was burning up with fever and his body was red all over.

Stepwilder knelt by his side. "How long you been sick, boy?"

"Three or four days, I reckon."

"You be sick to yore stomach, got a headache?"

"Yes sir. Both. I hurt all over."

He didn't have to tell the two men standing behind him, but he did.

"He's got Malaria. Them skeeters done it to him. I got some quinine, but don't know if it will do any good. He's purty bad." He turned and walked toward the cook wagon where he kept his medicine.

Donagon and Maxwell did not sleep well that night, worrying about Henry. They curled up in their bedrolls and left him alone through the night. At first light, they woke and looked in his direction. His body was no longer red as it had been. He appeared to be sleeping peacefully. Instead of waking him, they went to the building looking for something to eat.

While they sat with Boudreau and Rankin, Stepwilder stood in the doorway and waved to the trail boss. He whispered something to him, and then both looked at the two boys at the table.

"You boys check on Henry this morning?"

"No sir. He was sleeping, so we left him alone."

Both men hung their head. Boudreau spoke softly. "He weren't asleep. Henry's gone." He choked on his words.

"No! He can't be He was okay yesterday. He's got to be alright!" Bud yelled out.

"Sorry, son."

Donagon's expression did not change. He had mourned a father and mother, and vowed he would not do that again.

_____ ..... _____

Little Henry Jones was laid to rest under a cypress tree near the bank of the Atchafalaya Basin. After a moment of prayer, Boudreau stepped back away from the mound of earth covering the body.

"Let's move em out, boys. We burning daylight." He almost choked on the last word out of his mouth.

After another week of slow moving, the herd came upon a small village of French speaking people. Lavonia was the name. Boudreau seemed to know the town leaders and spoke their language fluently. When they were ready to leave, Stepwilder had with him a box filled with seasoning from the village.

Another five days and they were coming around the east end of the basin. It was time to turn the herd south toward the gulf. Boudreau knew he was getting close to his destination. From here to New Orleans, they would be on firmer ground until they got close to Lake Pontchatrain.

Donagon and Maxwell had little to say to the other men. They were missing their friend. As a result, they didn't pay enough attention to the terrain around them. They did not see the dozen war painted Indians who were slipping out of the trees and surrounding the remuda.

When Donagon turned to see where Maxwell was, he felt the sting of an arrow slice through his right side. He had no time to yell a warning to Bud. He was pulled from the saddle and an Indian replaced him. He had no way of knowing that the same had happened to Bud. There was not a sound as the redskins slowly drove the remuda into the trees and out of site of the point riders. Stepwilder was too busy planning what he would use the seasoning for, to notice.

Just as they had come, the band of Indians disappeared into the surrounding countryside. They rode slowly through the cedar and cypress trees for another four hours. It was getting dusk when they saw the glow of fires in the distance showing the hostiles the way home.

They threw the boys into a shelter made of pine boughs and cypress limbs. They left them alone in the dark, with no help for their wounds. It was the first chance they had to talk.

"You okay, Bud?"

"Yeh. They just nicked me. How about you?"

Arrow in my side. It hurts some. I need to pull it out, I guess."

"Can you see it?"

"No. It's too dark in here. I'll wait til my eyes get use to the dark."

21

"Let me know when you're ready. I'll help."

A voice on the outside of the wikiup sounded as though someone was having an argument. One of the voices did not sound like the same language they had heard from the Indians.

"Pourquoi avez-vous pris ces garçons?"(Why did you take those boys?)

Suddenly someone was opening the pine needle flap on the wikiup.

"Je m'excuse. Parlez-vous Français?"

They looked at him inquisitively.

"Do you speak English?"

"Who are you?"

"Ah. Mon ami. You are American."

"Who are you?" Donagon asked again.

"I am Joseph. I am the chief of this band. They are the Attakapas. I have been here eleven years. I was a priest, until the mission was abandoned. Then they made me their chief."

"What do they want with us?"

"They are man eaters. I suppose you looked inviting. Oh, but don't worry. I won't let them eat you. I will send you back to your cows."

"What about our horses?" Bud asked. "Mister Boudreau ain't going to like us losing them horses."

"I suppose I could let you take part of them back with you. They do need to get something to eat out of this. You or the horses."

_____ ….. _____

Boudreau had stopped the movement of the herd to search for his remuda and the young wranglers. He had the drovers search up and down both sides of the trail until it was too dark to see. He was puzzled how two boys and fifty horses could just disappear into thin air.

"That's it boys. We'll start looking again in the morning. Let's get some sleep."

At first light, Stepwilder had coffee brewing, beans, and biscuit ready. All the drovers were ready to get back on the trail of the disappearing boys. They needed those horses to finish the drive.

Just as they were getting started and Boudreau was telling them where to look, the two boys came out of the trees herding half their horses ahead of them.

Boudreau nor any of the drovers could speak. It was as if the remuda had just appeared. Donagon raised his hand into the air, then slowly slipped from the saddle and fell unconscious to the ground.

Chapter 3

So they signaled to their partners in the other boat for them
to come help them. And they came and filled both of the boats,
so they began to sink. Luke 5:7

Stepwilder was pushing on a wooden arrow shaft
when Donagon woke up. The pain brought him back
into a temporary consciousness. Then he was out
again. Bud Maxwell had only to put a bandage over
his flesh wound. He was left to explain to Boudreau
what had happened.

24

"I heard tell of somebody like that Joseph fellow. I thought it was just a tall tale. I reckon we had better keep on the lookout, in case they come back. He turned to yell at the top hand.

" Rankin, double the nighthawk til we get to New Awlins. Can't be losing no more of them cayuses. Watch the herd! Them redskins like to eat beef!"

It was another two days before Donagon was awake enough to know where he was.

"Better eat some of this here beef broth. You ain't had nothing to eat in two or three days." Stepwilder had been watching and waiting for him to wake. He sipped a little of the broth and went back to sleep.

Another three days passed before he was finally aware of what was going on around him.

"He saw Bud sitting by the fire looking at him. "Where are the horses?"

"We got back with half of em. Boudreau ain't too happy. He put two of them drovers to watching the remuda. I been helping Stepwilder look after you this last week."

"How far we from New Orleans?"

"Rankin said we'll be there in about another week."

"Don't think I'm going to drive no more cows over this way. What you going to do when we hit New Orleans?"

"I reckon I'll find something else to do too. I ain't no cowhand neither!"

———— ….. ————

Like Rankin had said, they were on the outskirts of the bayou city in another week. When they had found the stockyards and settled the herd in, Boudreau went into town and got cash money to pay off the drovers and wranglers. As soon as they were paid, all of them went looking for what the town had to offer. There was not much for two thirteen year old boys to do.

Soon enough they found their way to the banks of the Mississippi River, and fascinated by all the activity. They sat and watched for hours as black men loaded and unloaded ships moored at the docks. One long paddle wheeler caught their eye and both boys thought of it at the same time. Donagon was the first to voice his idea.

"I think I'm going to take a ride on one of them boats."

"Me too. Reckon they'll pay us to do that?"

"I reckon we can go ask."

Ask they did. Both hired on to the Delta Queen, a sixty feet stern wheeler headed up river to take a load of supplies to Vicksburg, Mississippi. Other than supplies for cotton farmers, the payload of the Queen was river gamblers. Donagon and Maxwell watched in awe as the men sat for hours at a table and dealt cards to one another, then bet on what they held. It looked like a fast way to make money or to lose it.

One of the gamblers, a tall man wearing a fancy suit and top hat took a shine to the two boys watching him take money from the others.

"What you younguns looking for?"

"Nothing. We was just watching. How do you win all that money like that?" Bud asked.

"I can show you, real easy. You really want to learn."

"Yes sir, I surely would like to learn. What you call that?"

"That is poker, my young friend. I can teach you all the ins and outs of that game. Before long, you'll be winning big money same as me."

We ain't done work yet, but when the captain lets us off, we sure do want to learn how to do that poker!"

"I'm in cabin number six, down them stairs over yonder." They followed his pointing finger. "Come on down."

It was near dark when the captain turned them loose from their daily chores. Making their way down the steps, they found a door with a six on it. Donagon knocked lightly and a voice called out. "Come on in!"

Bud pushed against the door and it squeaked open, revealing a well-lit room with a table in the middle. The gambler sat with another man who was dressed almost in identical clothing. There were two empty chairs on either side.

"Come on in, boys. Have a seat. We'll show you how to play this game. This is my partner, Mister James. My name is Johnson. "

They boys sat facing each other between the two gamblers

"Now this is how you do it boys. Pay close attention. You have to put your money on the table. I will deal the cards. Want take no time to show you how it's done."

He was right. It took no more than an hour to show the two youngsters how to lose all the money they had earned after two months of driving longhorns across a mosquito infested land.

"Well, that's it for today, boys. Come back tomorrow for lesson two."

"What about our money?" Bud asked.

"Why, boy. Didn't you know? You have to pay to learn this game."

"But that's all the money we have."

"Had, my boy. You just paid for your first poker lesson."

Donagon and Maxwell sat stunned. All of their money had been lost and they were in a strange place far from home. They had no real home, but San Antonio was what they knew.

"Goodnight, boys. It's time I got some sleep. See you tomorrow." The tall one pointed to the door.

In a state of shock, they walked out onto the deck. All they could hear was the monotonous slapping of wheels as they churned against the water.

"Now what we going to do?" Bud asked.

"I reckon we better go back to San Antone."

Not me. I'm going to learn how to play that game and get my money back."

"Suit yourself, Bud. I'm going back to Texas, if I have to walk all the way."

———————— ….. ————————

Four days later, the Delta Queen docked at a long pier in Vicksburg. Donagon could not wait to get his feet back on dry land once again. He walked down the gangway and stepped on Mississippi soil. He turned to see Bud Maxwell leaning on a rail on the upper deck.

He waved and turned to go, then looked back and saw Bud eyeing the two gamblers who had beat them out of all their money.

Donagon found a young black boy on the edge of town, who was pulling a short boat ashore.

"You reckon you could give me a ride to the other side of that river?"

"I reckon so. Sho is a long way cross there, but I takes you across. Better hurry fo my master come back. He want let me."

Donagon stepped into the small boat and an hour later, he was striding his way back across the swamps of Louisiana on his way to Texas.

He had walked for five days without food, and drinking water from streams. He came upon a plantation north of a town called Baton Rouge. Here he found a man dressed in a white suit with a wide brimmed Panama hat sitting in a rocking chair on the long front veranda. He looked over the top of a newspaper as Donagon approached.

"Where you come from, boy. You look kinda hungry."

"I am, sir. Could you spare a bite to eat. I ain't ashamed to work for it."

"Where you headed, boy?"

"On my way to Texas, sir. Sure am hungry."

"Well, now. You just hold your horses. I don't give food to just anybody. Where you coming from?"

"From New Orleans, sir."

"Sure you ain't from Vicksburg?"

"Donagons heart jumped. *How would he know where he come from?*

29

"I was just reading in this paper where a boy bout your age killed two of them river gamblers and robbed them."

His heart really jumped when he heard that.

"Reckon it couldna been you though. Says here, they hung that boy. Don't know what this old world coming to. Next thing you know, them darkies'll be wanting to be free like me and you. Tasha! Bring this here youngun some vittles!" He shouted to a wide screened door over his shoulder. Shortly an older black woman came out holding a chunk of corn bread and a glass of cool milk.

"Ya'll wants anything Massa?"

"Not now, Tasha. Make sure this boy is well fed, and show him where he can sleep for tonight. He's headed to Texas, you know. He got a long walk. Give him some food to take with him in the morning."

"Yassuh."

When Donagon had finished his milk and cornbread, she came back to light a lantern on the porch.

"Massa say put you in one dem rooms upstairs. Come on with me."

He followed her up the stairs and fell into a feather bed with clean white sheets for the first time in his life. It took him only seconds to fall into a deep sleep. When he woke, the sun was streaking through white fluffy curtains and falling across his face. At first, he did not know where he was and sat up straight in the bed. It finally dawned on him where he had slept. He was well rested and ready to get back on the road to home.

Making his way down the stairs, he saw the black woman sweeping the wide foyer with a big straw broom.

"Bout time ya'll wakes up. Massa Dawson done gone to check on them field hands. Told me to feed you and send you on yo way."

He ate ham and eggs, and large hot biscuits til he was about to bust.

"Land sakes, young'un. You sho gonna bust yo stomach. Best get on outa here, fore Massa come back. He make you work for all you done et!"

Donagon thanked the woman who had fed him and made his way down a long winding lane and onto a wider dirt road. He stopped to check the sun, then turned so it would be at his back and walked in the direction of Texas.

His mind went back to what the man had said about the two river gamblers killed. It was almost certain in his mind who had done it. That meant his only friend left in the world, had hung. He was all alone, now with no place to call home. All that mattered to him now was to get back to Texas.

He had to be on his toes as he made his way across the swampy land. It was not as bad as it had been on the way across the south end of the state. Instead of the Atchafalaya basin, there were rolling hills like in Texas. He was careful to stay away from towns and villages except to find something to eat.

After three weeks of long walking days, and nights where he had to find places to hide and sleep, he finally saw the Sabine River ahead. There was a ferry crossing the river with an old black man polling it back and forth. There was a small shack on the bank of the river, and several people lined up in wagons awaiting their turn to cross.

He slipped off into the trees and sat scanning the riverbank for a way to cross without getting on the ferry. It was early afternoon and he would have to wait until dark to cross so no one saw him. Sitting in the trees watching, he saw two women building fires and begin cooking meals for their families. It was all he could do, to stop from asking for something to eat. It had been three days since he had eaten last. Suddenly, from somewhere behind him he heard a small voice.

"Whatcha doing?"

He wheeled around to see a small girl of about eight or nine standing behind him. How she got there, he had no idea. At the same time, he heard a woman yell.

"John, Jenny is not in the wagon. I left her in there asleep! She's gone!"

Chapter 4

If anyone is hungry, let him eat at home, so that you will
not come together for judgment. The remaining matters I will
arrange when I come. 1 Corinthians 11:34

Donagon realized where the girl had gone. She
was standing right behind him. Before he knew what
was happening, he heard his own voice calling to the
woman.
"Here she is ma'am."

The woman and her husband whirled around to see where the voice came from, and then both ran to get the little girl.

"Who are you? What are you doing with Jenny?"

"I don't know no Jenny."

"Jenny, what are you doing out here?"

"I saw this boy, momma. He was just sitting here, so I come to see."

"Who are you, son?" This time it was the man speaking.

"I am David Donagon. I am going back to Texas. I was on a cattle drive to New Orleans."

"Where is your horse?"

"I don't have a horse."

"You walked from New Orleans?"

"Yes sir." Donagon did not want to tell the man he had come from Vicksburg.

"How far are you going?"

"I am going to San Antonio. That is my home town."

"Do you know the way?"

"Yes sir." He lied because he had never been this way before, but wanted a ride.

"We are going to Austin, then west. If you show us the way, you can ride with us."

"Yes sir. I will do that."

"John!"

"Hush, Mary. I have said all that needs saying. This boy looks like he could use a meal." He turned and walked back to the wagon, followed by his wife and daughter. Donagon hesitated for a minute and then followed them to the fire where a pot of beans smelled so good.

"Sit, young man." Mary picked up a tin plate and filled it with beans and passed it to him." I am Mary

Steinke. You have met my husband John and my daughter, Jenny." She was terse and to the point.

The old black man came around the wagon and spoke to John Steinke.

"That's all for tonight, Mister. You be first in the morning. Done too dark to cross that river."

The man looked at his wife, and then shook his head. "I reckon one more night won't hurt none. We will go to Texas tomorrow."

John Steinke had uprooted his wife and child from a Mississippi farm to go to Texas, looking for a better life. He had heard of how Stephen Austin was giving land grants to new settlers. He had heard that all a man had to do was make it to Austin. There his dreams would come true. Tomorrow, he would step on Texas soil and be on his way.

_____ ….. _____

The air was beginning to take on a slight chill. It was fall of eighteen thirty seven, and Sam Houston had already claimed victory over the Mexican army under Santa Anna, more than a year earlier.

First light and Donagon woke from a sound sleep with a full belly for the first time in days. Mary Steinke was already at the fire making coffee and fresh hot biscuits. The odor of fatback was what had wakened him. He sat up and watched the woman for a minute, until she spoke.

"Well, son, you going to eat or sleep all day?"

"I'm ready to eat, ma'am." He got up from his place under the wagon.

This time the woman smiled at him as she handed him a plate.

"John, breakfast is ready." She called to her husband who was tending the team of four horses. He came to join his family and their new traveling companion.

"Where are your Ma and Pa, son?' he asked.

"My Pa got killed in the war. My Ma, she just passed."

"Do you have any family?"

"No sir. My Ma's Pa turned her away cause she married my Pa."

"I spect you will be glad to get back home."

"Yes sir."

The ferry operator came around the front of the wagon.

"Be ready to put you on the ferry in twenty minutes, Mister. Best get ready, or move out the way, so's them folks behind you can go."

"We're ready. Mary put out the fire while I get the team ready. Son, you know horses?"

"Yes sir. I was a wrangler on that cattle drive."

"Good for you. Want to give me a hand?"

"Yes sir."

John Steinke was amazed at the knowledge of horses by a boy that young. It was only minutes before they were leading the team onto the ferry. A short time later, they rolled off onto the Texas side for the first time. For Donagon it was a homecoming, or it would be if he had a home.

"Ever heard of the San Saba River, son?"

"I've heard of it. Never been there."

"That's where we're headed. We got a homestead out there. Give to us by Stephen Austin from the Mexican government. Six hundred forty acres. Ought to make a good farm. I hear tell its good bottom land."

"Yes sir." Donagon knew nothing of farming and was sure he did not want to know. He was not sure what he would do when he got back to San Antonio, or if he would even go there. He had only been to Austin once in his young life on a trip with his father when he was ten. He didn't remember much of that.

It took another week of slow rolling in a loaded wagon. The Steinke had all their worldly possessions with them. Mary Steinke had refused to leave her good dishes and silver.

Salado Creek was a narrow winding creek with sulphur deposits along its banks. When they drew near John Steinke realized that the dwellings he saw along the creek were Indian teepees. He reached for his old Sharps rifle and laid it across his lap. It was too late to turn aside. He pulled back on the reins and stopped.

"What is it, John?" His wife was inside the wagon and had not seen the village.

"Stay put, Mary. It's Indians."

As he spoke the words, he saw one of the braves lift his hand in a friendly greeting.

"John?"

"They look friendly, Mary. I'll try to talk to them." He raised his own arm in greeting.

Donagon had never seen the tribe before and he did not know who they were. His only dealings with Indians was the tribe who wanted to eat him.

They rode slowly into the center of the village with youngsters following alongside the wagon. A tall brave came out of a teepee and stood waiting for them to stop.

"My name is Green Turtle. I am chief of this band. We are Tonkawa. We are friends with the white eyes."

John put his rifle away and cautiously stepped down from the wagon seat. The brave put out his arm and shook hands with their visitors. It was a very vigorous shake.

"It's okay, Mary. They are friends. Come on out."

Donagon had gotten down from the seat and followed by some boys. When the Tonkawa saw the blond hair of the woman and girl, they began to point and snicker. Most of their contact with whites was with part Mexicans who all had dark hair and eyes. Blond was new to them, as were the blue eyes.

Several of the Tonkawa women brought food and small birds that had baked over a hot fire. Ears of corn were roasted and handed to them wrapped in the husk. It was a feast for folks who had survived on beans and bread.

After they had their fill, the chief asked where they were going.

John spoke in slow English. "San Saba. Do you know it?"

"Know San Saba." He pointed to the west. "Over many hills. Many moons. We show you."

"You show us?"

"We show!"

They stayed three more days on the banks of Salado creek, and the Tonkawa chief sent two braves to show them the way to the San Saba River. The terrain changed to a little steeper rolling hills and the countryside was getting more difficult to travel.

After five days of rolling over the hills, they spotted the Colorado River and made camp on the west bank after finding a shallow place to cross. John Steinke was content to take his time to get to the San Saba, where he would build a new life for his family.

He had spent hours talking to the young boy he had found on the Sabine River. Donagon did not talk much, but he had figured out that he could have a family with these folks. Mister Steinke had asked if he would like to go with them, to the San Saba River, and after thinking about it those three days with the Tonkawa, he had agreed. Now he was on his way to the only real home he had known since his father died.

When they reached the Colorado, the two braves pointed them to a fork in the river and one of them grunted and spoke slowly the words,

"San Saba, we go now." They abruptly turned and began retracing their footprints back the way they came.

The Steinke and their ward were all alone in a wilderness and hoped they could find their way up the river to a fork with Brady creek. That was where their homestead would be.

They set out at first light and followed the winding river for four more days. Steinke was just about to give up when Donagon pointed ahead.

"Looks like a stream dumping into the river."

"By Golly, I think you're right. Mary look! I think we are home!"

It took them another two hours to maneuver the team into a grove of trees just upstream of the creek fork.

"This is where we will build a cabin, Mary. See, there's a flat place for your vegetable garden. David, we still got three hours of light. We can cut a couple of trees while the women cook a meal. We must celebrate tonight!"

Excitement overcame John Steinke. He had looked the river bottom over as they rode the wagon along, and knew it was good, rich soil.

It was early fall and the air was turning colder, as John Steinke and his new helper cut logs and built walls for a cabin. The man seemed obsessed and worked from sunup til sundown every day, trying to finish their home before it was too cold.

In the days and months to come, Donagon would come to realize that John Steinke was a hardworking man and expected no less from others.

They finished the cabin and had a roof on it before a first light snow fell. They would find that it did not snow much along the San Saba. Their first winter was a mild one and they were able to build a barn and corral before spring.

Mary had her husband, before Easter, break ground for her garden, and was ready to plant the seeds she had brought from Mississippi. Things were going great for them and they had not seen hide nor hair of any hostiles.

Mary's garden was up and blooming and John had started plowing ground near the river. Donagon worked hard alongside the man, lifting rocks from under and in front of the plow. The land was black and fertile and Steinke knew he would have a good crop of corn by summer. Game was plentiful and they had already filled the smokehouse with enough meat to last them all winter.

Donagon found himself gazing over the horizon and wondering what was around the next bend of the river. He was very fond of his new family, but began to wonder if he was destined to be a farmer. His mind was always going to the next bend of the river. He was becoming a restless soul. Donagon kept his feelings to himself. He did not want to hurt the family that had taken him in.

Chapter 5

There is only one Lawgiver and Judge, the One who is able
to save and to destroy: but who are you who judge your
neighbor? James 4:12

For three years, Donagon wondered what was
outside their little world. Occasionally someone
would stop by and visit for a while and talk about the
outside world and what was happening in Texas.

"You folks better be on the lookout for Comanche. They're on the warpath. Seems like somebody killed thirty three of them at San Antone."

"Why were they killed?"

"They brung hostages to trade, and somehow it got out of hand, and them government men started shooting. Killed them thirty-three like I said. Now them Comanch is on the warpath. They looking for blood."

That was the first they had heard about the Indians being on the warpath. Another month went by and another man stopped for water.

"You folks hear about that Comanche raid down on the coast. Heard tell five hundred of them red devils attacked a little town called Linville. Stole a whole bunch of goods and horses. They may be headed back this way."

John Steinke started carrying a rifle with him to the fields. He and Donagon were always looking to the tree lines for movement. Soon, another man stopped on his way to the Big Bend Mountains.

"Texas rangers and some of them Tonkawa Indians caught up with them Comanch at Plum creek. Heard they might near wiped them devils out."

Donagon heard the conversation and asked. "What are Texas ranger?"

"They's a bunch of lawmen the governor brung together to fight them Injuns and Mexicans. Heard they works directly for the governor."

Donagon started thinking about the Rangers.. He never did take to farming much. He had given it three years, and didn't think that was what he wanted to be.

Late one evening when they were leaving the field, he approached John Steinke.

"Mister Steinke, I think I'll be moving on."

"Moving on. Where will you go, son?"

"I been thinking about them Rangers."

"Well, I can tell you don't like farming much."

"No sir, I don't. You been good to me. I don't want Miss Steinke or Jenny to know til I'm gone. Is that okay?"

"I will tell them after you leave. When do you think you'll begin this journey?"

"I think I'll leave in the morning if it's okay with you. We bout got things caught up."

"You know them women folk going to miss you a lot."

"Yes sir. I'm going to miss them a lot too."

"Well, you've earned a horse and saddle. You pick out one you want and take it."

"Thank you, sir."

Before daylight, Donagon was leading his mount out of the barn, wearing the new trousers and shirt, Mary Steinke had made for him. He quietly walked around the barn and past the corral before throwing a leg over and sitting up in the saddle. He turned and looked back at the house where a lantern had just been lit. He would miss the people who had taken him in and given him a home.

"John Steinke walked into the kitchen as Mary was pouring him a cup of coffee. She picked up another cup to fill for the boy.

"No need for that."

She stopped and looked at her husband. "Is David not drinking coffee this day?"

"David is gone, Mary. He left this morning before you were up."

Jenny walked into the room rubbing sleep from her eyes.

"What did you say about David, Papa?" She saw the look on her mother's face.

"David is gone. He did not want to be a farmer."

"Where did he go?" A tear formed in the corner of her eye. She had gotten feelings for David Donagon beyond those of a sister or friend. She had never said anything, but the feeling was there.

——————— ….. ———————

David Donagon rode into Austin on a cool, fall, morning. He rode down the street until he saw a sign that read. *Republic of Texas Rangers' office*. He stepped down and walked up the two steps and through a white double door, into a wide foyer. A man seated at a desk in one corner looked up as he entered.

"Help you with something?"

"Yes sir. How do I become a ranger?"

"Raise your right hand and repeat after me. I swear to uphold the laws of the Republic of Texas, and will arrest or shoot anybody who don't."

Donagon repeated what the man had said. The man behind the desk rummaged in a drawer and found a badge.

"Sergeant in that room yonder will give you your orders." He pointed to a door.

Donagon walked down the hall and tapped lightly on the door.

"You got to knock louder than that. Sarge don't hear so good."

45

He knocked again, harder.

A booming voice yelled. "Come!"

He opened the door and stepped inside.

"How old are you boy?"

"Sixteen, sir."

"Well, I reckon you'll have to do. You know how to shoot? I see you ain't wearing a gun!"

"Yes sir. I can shoot a rifle."

"You got one of them?"

Yes sir. I got an old Sharp. Mister Steinke give me."

"Who? Never mind, be here at first light. I got to send a patrol out. Lord help me!"

Donagon seated himself on the steps before daylight the next morning. Three other boys approached him.

"I'm Bobby Clemens."

"I'm Dave Donagon."

"I'm Josh Benton."

"I'm Fred Fuller."

They all shook hands and Josh asked. "How long ya'll been rangers?"

"Since last night." They all said in unison.

The sergeant heard the voices and opened the door.

"What's all that racket about?"

"We ready to go, Sarge." Fred said.

"Yeh, I'll bet you are. Saddle up and follow me. We got word them Comanche is raiding west of here."

All four of the new rangers excitedly threw a leg over and rode after the Sarge. Not until they rode out of town, did Donagon realize where they headed. They were backtracking the trail he had rode from the San Saba River the day before. His heart raced as he thought about the Steinke family and their farm.

At mid- morning, they rode up on a burning house, and saw three people lying in front with arrows in their backs. Two men and one woman had lost their hair. They buried the bodies and then rode on. There were two other farms burned to the ground, and the next one would be the Steinke place.

An hour later Donagon saw smoke rising above where the cabin had been. When they were closer, he saw John Steinke slumped over the water trough in front of the cabin. Mary Steinke was sitting in a chair on the porch with two arrows in her chest. Both had blood running down their faces from the scalping. He jumped from his horse and ran to the front of the house. He had already helped bury nine people today, and he did not want to have to bury the people who had taken him in. He did not see Jenny anywhere, so he ran to the barn. She was not there. He checked around back by the corral and no Jenny. All the horses were gone. Most of the other stock either killed or taken. Donagon leaned against the side of the barn so the others could not see him, and puked his guts out. He laid his head against the barn and sobbed uncontrollably.

When he had gathered himself, he walked to where the others were digging one more, shallow grave.

"Did you find the girl?"

"What girl?"

"Jenny. She is a girl, twelve years old."

"You know these folks, son?" The Sarge asked.

"Yes sir. They were my adopted family. I just left yesterday to join the rangers. I should have stayed."

"Then, we would be burying you too. I reckon they took the girl. Comanche are big on hostages. Like to trade or sell them to the highest bidder."

"We got to go find her, Sarge."

"We'll track them for a while. Looks like a big raiding party. We may need help."

"I can't let them get away with her, Sarge. We got to go find her."

"We'll do what we can."

They rode out and followed the San Saba westward, trying to pick up the trail of the renegades. They did not have to look long. The Comanche were not trying to hide their tracks. The Indians stayed right along the riverbank and were only about three hours ahead of the rangers. The sarge pulled rein and told the men.

"We'll make camp here."

"But, Sarge. It still daylight!" Donagon did not want to stop.

"We got to rest these horses and our self. We'll catch up with them tomorrow."

"But, Jenny!"

"She won't be no different tomorrow than today. Them devils gonna do anything to her, it's already been done. If it's any help, they usually save their captured women to trade."

It was not any consolation to Donagon. He wanted to keep after them. He did not sleep any that night. His thoughts were on a little girl that he had grown to love like a sister. Sometime before daylight, he dozed and woke to the smell of coffee brewing. While the others ate hardtack and fatback, he saddled his horse.

"I'm going to ride ahead, Sarge. Look for tracks."

"Suit yourself, son. They'll still be there when we get done."

He rode out alone and followed the tracks of a moving band of hostiles along the San Saba. He

48

finally saw the dust of a group of horses in the distance and kicked up his mount to gain on them. By the middle of the afternoon, he was in sight of a band of Comanche warriors. He had caught up with the bunch that had taken Jenny. Knowing better than to ride up on them, he hung back and waited until they were ready to make camp. He could see some people who were obviously not Indians by their dress. He was sure one of them must be the girl.

Waiting until full dark and the Indians had fires, he tied his horse and crawled on his hands and knees to the outer perimeter of the camp. He could see some captives tied in a circle with their hands behind their back. He crept closer for a better look.

Pulling his knife, he began to crawl slowly to where the hostages were. He could get to Jenny and cut her free and both of them would be off.

Jenny raised her head at the sign of a movement and found herself looking straight into the eyes of the boy she loved. He had come to save her. Just as she saw him, she also saw a Comanche Indian brave creeping up behind him. Donagon was so intent on setting her free, he neither saw nor heard what she saw.

A tomahawk raised high in the air and came down on the side of his head. He went unconscious just as he heard a gunshot somewhere in the distance.

The Sarge and the other three Texas rangers had caught up with Donagon and the Comanche just in time. A short gun battle ensued and the rangers were beat back into a cluster of rocks. The Comanche realized they were under attack, and they yanked their captives to their feet, and drug them into the darkness.

If it had not been for the rangers, Donagon would have lost his scalp. Instead, the Comanche slinked off into the night, leaving him lying in a pool of blood.

Bobby Clemens of the Texas rangers had found death on his first assignment as a ranger. Fred Fuller wounded in the left arm. The Sarge, nor none of the others, expected the Comanche, would be armed with rifles, but they were. When they realized the Indians had slipped away in the dark, they went to check on the tomahawked ranger. He was still alive, but just barely.

The Sarge and Benton buried Clemens under a pile of rock, then helped Fuller mount his horse. They had bandaged Donagon's head and thrown him over his saddle. There was no need to go after the Comanche. They would have to ride back to Austin at first light. For now, they would ride a ways in the dark, just to make sure they were away from the Indians.

Chapter 6

Simon and his companion searched for him; they found him
and said to him, "Everyone is looking for you."
Mark 1:35, 36.

When Donagon came around, he was in a bed
with white sheets. His head was bandaged and
throbbing with pain. The door to his room closed and
no one else was there.

He looked around for a minute, and then fell asleep. His dreams took him back out on the trail in search of Jenny Steinke. When he awoke again it was light out and the sun was shining through his window. He tried to get out of the bed, but his head started spinning and he fell back.

Not knowing how long he had been there, he began to try to piece things together. The last thing he remembered was crawling toward Jenny in a Comanche war camp. Then he remembered the sharp pain on the side of his head. After that, there was nothing.

Muffled voices made him look to the door and wait for someone to come in. He didn't wait long. The Sarge and an older man swung the door open and walked into the room.

"Well, young man, I see you are awake. I bet you're hungry." It was the old bespectacled man speaking.

"How you doing, Donagon?" The Sarge asked.

"Head hurts some. How is Jenny?"

"Don't know that, boy!"

"Didn't we get her back?"

"Nope. You near got yourself killed. We hadn't showed up that Comanch would have scalped you. Fuller shot him."

"You mean we didn't get her. I was so close! Why didn't you get her back? She was right there!"

"So was a passel of Comanch. Near bout got us all killed, boy. Clemens did get it!"

"We got to get moving. We got to go find her!"

"You ain't going nowhere for a while. Ask the doc?"

"I'll go by myself. I can't leave her out there with Comanche. She's all alone! She needs my help!" Once again, he tried to get up, with the same results.

"Doc, how soon can I get up?"

"I'd say you need another three, four days. You was hurt bad, son. You lucky to be alive. Hadn't been for the Sergeant here you wouldn't be"

Two days later, he was trying to get up again and found he could stand for a few minutes. From that point, he stood up every hour and by the third day, he was walking around the building and out onto a small porch. He saw that he was only a block away from ranger headquarters.

On the morning of the fourth day, he left his room and strolled down the street. The desk corporal was surprised to see him.

"Sarge in there?"

No. He's out on patrol. Gone after a bank robber."

"Who's out there looking for Jenny?"

"Who?'

"His temper flared. "You don't know who Jenny is? Who's looking for them hostages the Comanche took."

"Nobody, I know of. That ain't the only thing rangers got to do!"

"Well, take the rangers and….."

He threw his badge on the desk and whirled around to leave, almost falling from a dizzy spell. Stopping for a minute, he righted himself and stomped down the steps.

_____ ….. _____

Donagon found the livery and saddled his horse. If no one had gone after Jenny, he would go it alone. He threw a leg over and rode out of Austin. He headed to the forks of the San Saba, and Brady creek. Jenny would not be there, but it was a place to start.

A week later, he rode onto the Steinke farm. He found the graves of John and Mary. Donagon stepped down and removed his hat. Standing there a flood of memories of the last three years ran through his mind. Promising the couple he would not quit before he had found Jenny, he took a walk around the place. David Donagon felt lost and was not sure what he should do. All he knew was that he had to try to get Jenny back. He had made that promise and he meant to keep it.

This time he would get what he was going after. He would find Jenny and bring her safely away from the Comanche. He had promised the Steinke. With a feeling of anger, he threw a leg over his saddle and rode down the river.

Following the San Saba until it joined with the Concho River, he saw that the Comanche had turned north and followed the Concho. He found their trail and followed it. He had never been in this country before, so he rode slow and cautious.

It had been more than three weeks since he had last seen the girl and wasn't sure if she was still alive. It was late in the day when he rode up on the fork of the Concho and Lacy Creek. He saw the glow of low fire and pulled rein.

Donagon dismounted and continued on foot. In the light of the flickering flames, he saw a single figure seated by the fire with a cup in his hand. His other hand was on the butt of a six-gun.

"Come on in, stranger, but keep yore hands where I can see em."

Donagon lifted his hands and walked slowly into the firelight.

"Have a cup."

Donagon poured a cup and eyed the old man seated in front of him. "Names Donagon."

"Please to make yore acquaintance. I'm Ben Walters. Where you headed, young man?"

"Been tracking a bunch of Comanche. Got a girl I'm going to take back."

"Blue eyes, blond? Purty little thing?"

"Yes! How did you know?"

"Ran into them a week ago up at them Comanche springs. They was having a trade fair. Least, that's what I calls em."

"What's that mean?"

"Them Comanch bring all their hostages to the springs, and then sells them back to their family. Family don't come, they sell them to whoever got the trade goods. Come close to buying one of them ladies myself. Got out bid by a string of shells."

"What happened to the girl? Was she still there?"

"Last I seen, she was."

"Which way did they go from there?" Donagon felt he was close to finding Jenny.

"I reckon they headed to the Nations. Since Andy Jackson passed that Indian Removal act in thirty, governments trying to get them all moved up yonder. Some of them Comanch just plain stubborn. I don't reckon I blame them, though. They was here long before we was."

"Do they take whites up there with them?"

"Some. Them is most likely renegades. They leave the Nation to make raids, then go back to get fed. Can't blame em. They was here first! I reckon I'll get some shut eye. Headed to them Big Bend Mountains tomorrow. Hope you find that girl. Shore did look scared." The old man slid under a blanket and went to sleep.

The boy dozed some, and was awake before light. The old man was still sleeping when he saddled up and eased out of the camp. He was still at least four days from the springs, and the Comanche might still be there. Riding hard, he may be able to get there before they were gone. He kicked his horse and picked up the pace to a slow trot.

Late on the third day, he felt he was getting close. He had followed the Concho and the water seemed to be running a little faster. That meant the springs were running into it somewhere close by. By nightfall, he was almost there. In the far distance, he could barely see the glow of a low flame. He would wait until it was light enough to see the hostages, and most important, he had to keep an eye out for Indian guards.

At first light, he left his horse staked out by the river and eased toward the springs on foot. The sun was getting full above the horizon when he saw the fire near the edge of the water. It was not an Indian fire and there were no Comanche about. What he saw were two men sitting by the fire drinking coffee. He smelled fatback cooking in a fry pan.

"Coming in! Don't shoot!"

One of the men pulled a six-gun and turned in his direction.

"Come on! Keep yore hands up!"

Donagon stood up and walked slowly with his hands raised above his head.

"What you doing out here, young feller?"

"Trailing them Comanche. What are ya'll doing?"

"Them Comanch long gone. Ain't none of yore business what we doing!"

"Now, Jake. Ain't no harm in telling him we lawmen chasing them bandits robbed that bank in Abilene."

Jake got a funny look on his face. "Oh, reckon not." He smiled. "Pour yoreself a cup, partner."

"Thanks. How long them Comanche been gone?"

"We been here two days. They was gone when we got here. You can see where they was over yonder." He pointed to a circle of cold fire rings.

"Thanks for the coffee." Donagon stood to go. When he turned, he spotted a bank money bag sticking out of one of their saddle bags. He pretended not to see it and walked away.

Finding his horse, he mounted and rode away to the north. He reached into his saddlebag and pulled a coat out. The air suddenly took on a cold, dry feeling. He had lost all track of time and seasons.

It must be close to November, He thought, as he rode away from the two outlaws at the springs. By midday, the air had really gotten cold and there was a flurry of light snow beginning to fall. He was right on the edge of the Llano Atascosa and there was nothing to block the wind.

There was nothing in this part of the country but open plains. It was a cold, lonely place to be in the winter. By night, the snow was heavy and blowing hard. It was getting difficult for him to see. He had to keep wiping the snow from the eyes of his horse to keep going.

His horse stumbled and nearly fell, before he realized he was about to go off a high precipice. He pulled rein just in time and yanked his horses head around. He sat staring down into a deep ravine.

Dismounting, Donagon walked the edge until he saw a path going down into the canyon and led his horse down. Halfway down into the gorge, he found the snow a little less swirling. Just as it was getting dark, he saw an opening in the rock and saw that it was a cave. He led his horse into the opening and found himself in a cold, but dry place. He found enough sticks to build a fire.

He took the saddle from his horses back and rubbed him down. Partly to remove the snow and partly to warm the animal. He curled up by the fire and quickly fell asleep.

When he woke, the wind was howling across the canyon and it had piled deep along the edge of the cave. There was no way he could make it back up the canyon wall. He would have to stay put, until the snowstorm was over. He made a pot of coffee and put a fry pan on for fatback and biscuits. His thought went back to the times when Mary Steinke had taught him and Jenny how to make biscuits. It had been a fun time.

Still snowed in, three days later, it was too dangerous to try to climb back out of the gorge he found himself. He had cooked a pot of beans for himself, but he had nothing to feed his horse.

Finally, the snow began to slow to a light mist. It was a lot easier to see now, so he wondered out of the cave and tried to get his bearing. From where he stood, the canyon looked deep. When he looked up, he saw that he was no more than twenty or thirty feet from the rim. Making his way up on foot, he found a path out of the gorge, then went back and saddled his horse.

Instead of riding him, he led the hungry animal out of the cavern and along the path upward. When they had made it back onto flat ground, Donagon kicked around in the snow, and found a small patch of vegetation and showed it to his horse. He did not have to force the animal to eat. His horse kept pushing snow aside with his nose until he found more patches of food.

A lonely boy, quickly becoming a man, stood staring out into a vast field of white, wondering where he would go next in his quest for Jenny.

Chapter 7

Keep me as the apple of your eye; Hide me in the shadow
of your wings. Psalm 17:8

She had only caught a glimpse of him, before a
Comanche warrior killed him. Jenny had seen both
her parents die, and now the only other person in her
world was gone. She was jerked to her feet, and with
the other hostages, dragged off into the darkness.

They had spent a week at the place called Comanche Springs, and she had seen a hubbub of activity throughout the village. Indians of different tribes, walked among the captives, and white men too. All of them searched for their kin. After the third day, the hostages paraded in front of a group of men who seemed to be bidding on wares.

One at a time, they dragged the women off into the shadows. Jenny Steinke was one of the last to go. Not because of her looks, but because she was so young. Even the rough looking men from the mountains had some pride about them.

There was no conversation with her. The man who bought her for a string of beads said nothing. He simply untied her hands and pointed to a bareback horse tied with another one wearing a saddle and a pack animal. He hefted her up high enough to get her leg over the back and she threw her chin out and sat proud.

There was still no talk as he grabbed the reins and led the horses out of the village and turned south. There was a chill in the air as they rode away. A tear formed in her eyes when they passed near a river she thought to be the San Saba.

The coolness in the air did not last long. The farther south they traveled, the warmer it got. There was no one to talk to on the long days rides. Her new captor had little to say, and at night, he tied her hands to keep her from running away. She finally realized the river they had crossed was not the one near her home. She was lonely, and frightened, not knowing what was to become of her. For days, they kept a slow pace across the dry, desert landscape. Somewhere in the distance, a range of white capped peaks began to rise out of the parched floor.

Jenny, was only given water enough to keep her alive, and her diet was a daily ration of flat bread and beans. She smelled the coffee each time her abductor stopped for the night. It reminded her of the nights she sat around a fireplace with her Ma and Pa, smelling fresh brewed coffee mixed with the odor of her father's pipe.

Soon, they came upon another river and turned west to follow it toward the mountain peaks. For another week, they followed what she would learn was the Rio Grande river. Into the foothills they climbed until they turned to higher ascents and the snow caps drew nearer.

The higher they climbed, the colder the air became. Snow was falling more and more every day, and the man she followed had no sympathy for her freezing condition. He had pulled a buffalo robe from the pack animal and wrapped it around himself for protection from the blowing icy flakes.

Jenny Steinke had never been in the mountains and had never seen snow falling in sheets that covered everything. She shivered through the long days, and finally one day when they had stopped, the man threw a blanket over her as she laid trying to sleep on the cold ground. Grabbing it with both hands, she tried to cover her body but only got part of it done.

Finally falling into a shallow sleep, she heard a noise somewhere near, but did not move. The snow had covered her completely and whatever it was could not tell there was someone under the mound of snow. Through the night, the snow fell even harder, and a deep blanket of snow covered her. The heavier the snow, the warmer she became.

The frightened young girl slept until she could sleep no more. Jenny began to try to move around, wondering why the man had not awakened her. When she finally was able to remove the blanket from her head, she looked around for her captor. He was nowhere in sight. Slowly, she sat up, and brushed the snow away and looked around.

There was no one. The man was gone and so were his horses and pack animal. Jenny made it to her knees and found she was stiff from the cold. She pulled the blanket around her and took a couple of steps. Not knowing what else to do, she began to stumble through the snow. She had no idea where she was or how to get down from the mountains.

Snow was still falling and she had to squint into the cloudy sky to see a glimpse of sunlight. Putting one foot in front of the other, she methodically moved along. Her stomach was empty and there was no signs she would eat soon. Scooping handfuls of fresh snow, she managed to quench her thirst and fill part of the cavity in her belly.

Every so often, she would stop and gaze into the blowing snow, trying to see what lay in front of her. After several hours, she saw what she thought was the wall of a cabin. She stopped and stared until she had convinced herself that's what it was. Plodding along for another hour in the deep drifts, she finally made it to within reach of a large, heavy handle.

Standing for a minute to catch her breath, she pulled on the wooden block. At first, the door did not move, but she kept straining and tugging until she felt a slight movement.

Pulling hard and steady, she was able to ease the door open enough to squeeze though the small opening. Stepping inside she found herself in a cold, dark room. She stood for a while, trying to adjust her eyes, but the room got no lighter. Feeling her way around a wall, she stumbled, clinging closely to the logs, until she reached out and felt something that had a different texture. It was the stone of a fireplace.

Feeling her way, she found the hearth and an opening. Her nose detected a smoky odor and she guessed she was in front of the fire pit. She sat on the hearth and waited for her eyes to clear. It seemed like forever. Forms started taking shape and she began to recognize objects from her past. There was a rustic chair with rocker, which reminded her of home.

Jenny, taught by her father how to start a fire with two sticks, wondered if she could still remember. She looked around for the tools she needed and saw nothing in sight. Knowing she must find fire and heat or die from freezing, she slipped back through the opening and searched around in the increasing snow piles.

Down on her knees, she brushed the snow away near a tree and found a few small sticks. Farther away, she spotted a limb protruding from the snow. Slowly, she drug the limb inside and after several more trips into the cold snow had managed to have enough tinder to try to get a fire.

Piling smaller sticks first, she broke the limb into several smaller ones. It took a great deal of strength and effort. By the time she had everything in place, she was exhausted and had to sit and rest. Once more, she scanned the open room and saw things she had not seen before. There were shelves on both sides of the hearth with pots and pans hanging underneath. One was a blue porcelain coffee pot.

Back to the chore of building a fire, she formed a small pile of tender and began doing as her father had taught her. Furiously rubbing the sticks together, she knew that it would take time to create enough friction to set the tinder afire. In her weakened condition, she had to rest frequently. She tried not to stop long enough for the sticks to get cold, before she began again.

It seemed like forever before she saw a light smoldering in the tinder and when a wisp of smoke appeared, she blew softly. A small glow turned into a small flame and she slid it under the pile of wood.

For the first time in what seemed like weeks, Jenny Steinke felt a warmth penetrate her young body. When the fire had blazed high enough, she could see much better. She stood and walked around the room and finding her herself near the rocker, she sat and holding her head in her hands, began to sob uncontrollably.

Jenny had managed to find a place out of the weather, but she was all alone in the world. She had lost both her parents and the only friend she had ever had.

——————— ….. ———————

For years, a young white woman was hiding from anyone who came around her cabin. She had learned to trap animals for food and found a way to make fishing hooks and line to catch the numerous rainbow trout that swam in the high mountain streams. She had even learned the art of smoking fish, fowl, and meat to last her through the long cold winter months.

Jenny Steinke had resigned herself to never having contact with the world outside her mountaintop. She had found a cave in the side of the mountain not far from her cabin and had spent many months outfitting it and making it a hideaway when she heard or saw anyone coming. She could wipe out her tracks from the cabin to the cave, even with deep snow on the ground.

The only way off this mountain was to walk or allow someone to help her find the way. She had lost trust in anyone in the human race and had grown used to being alone in her own world. She had learned to venture outside her small world in order to find food. The first signs of spring on her first year in the mountains, she had retraced her trail back to where she had last seen the man who had brought her to this place.

Unknown to her, under the deep snow, when she woke from a deep sleep was an arrow, riddled, body. When she found it in the spring, she could tell by the clothes who it had been. Apparently, Indians had killed him and taken his horses. They had not found her in her hibernation under the snow. Never again did she travel that far from the safety of her cabin home.

It was on a particularly cold winter that she had heard voices of white men above the cold wintry wind. Just in time, she had left the cabin and made her way to her hidden cave. For four days, she had stayed hidden from view while the men occupied her cabin.

She watched as smoke plumed from her chimney and sat by a warm fire of her own in the cave. No one could see the smoke from her fire. It sifted through the back of the cave and exited through a small opening in the rear.

She watched while the two men led their pack animals and saddle horses into the cabin out of the cold. It appeared that one of the men was much more susceptible to the cold. He seemed to be complaining about the frigid weather. Watching from a distance for four days, she had on several occasions, thought about confronting them. She wondered what it would be like to hear the sound of white voices up close. She had listened to the muffled sounds from a distance, but could not determine what they were saying.

Jenny decided to stay in her cave and not risk the possibility of the white men seeing her. She sat by her fire and ate smoked fish and jerky she had made. Every few hours she would look at the cabin through the trees to see if there was still a wisp of smoke rising into the sky.

It was becoming more and more of a temptation for her to walk to the cabin and see what the two men were. That did not mean she had to spend time with them.

She could sit at the entrance to the cave and gaze through the trees and watch for activity. The two men did not wonder far from the cabin, in fact they hardly came out at all.

On the morning of the fourth day, she watched the cabin door open and one of the men led their mounts and pack animals out into the cold air. It was beginning to snow heavily again as they stepped into their saddles and turned to ride away from her cabin. She was glad to see them go. Now she could go back into her home.

She eased out of the cave and walked gingerly in the fresh falling snow. Standing by the door of the cabin, she watched the two riders slowly move back into the direction they had come.

It had been several years since she had seen anyone up this close or heard the sound of voices. She had made sure over the years that she spoke her language, even if she was the only one who heard her.

She took one last look at the backs of the riders as they disappeared over the horizon. A sudden pang in her heart gave her a lonely feeling. Going back into the cabin, she sat for a while and cried. *Why, had she been left all alone in the world? Why had she lost all the people she loved? Why was God punishing her this way?*

Chapter 8

Have you entered the storehouses of the snow, Or, have you
seen the storehouses of the hail, Job 38:

He had lost track of the Comanche in the deep
snow. All he could do was keep moving north toward
the Nations, and hope he would cross their path again.
Some of the drifts were higher than he was tall and it
was tough going for his horse. They kept plodding
along, looking for some sign of the Indians, or at this
point, any other human.

Near dusk, there was a faint glow of light off in the distance. He was about to make camp, but decided to ride on and see what the source of the light was. Out of the west Texas flatlands rose a cluster of buildings. There appeared to be five or six buildings, almost as if there was a town there.

Donagon rode between them. There were four in a row on one side, and two others across from them. There was the faint sound of music coming from the one that had a lantern in the window. He stepped down and walked across a wooden porch to a heavy door closed against the cold weather.

Just as he reached for the door latch, someone from inside pushed against it. He stepped back and waited. When the door swung open, a person wrapped in a large heavy buffalo robe walked out into the cold. His appearance startled them and they stopped.

"Well, don't just stand there. Come in out of the cold."

He could tell it was a woman's voice. She stepped back inside and waved him in.

"Why, you're just a young'un!"

"I'm cold and hungry ma'am. Any food here?"

"We can probably round up a piece of meat and a tater. Hey, Sam! Get this young'un something to eat. I reckon he's old enough to eat meat."

"Ma'am before I eat. Is there somewhere to put my horse?"

"You passed it! Building next door is a livery. Door's closed cause it's cold. Just open the door and go on in. Owner won't be there before morning, but that's okay."

He took his horse to the stable, and rubbed him down and fed him some hay. When he returned to the saloon, Sam was bringing a steak out of a back room.

"I bet that smells good to you, don't it son?"

"Yes sir."

"Well, sit down and get yourself some warm food"

The woman who had invited him in came and sat next to him.

"What you doing out in that cold? Where did you come from?"

"I come from Austin. I'm looking for a band of murdering Comanche. They got a girl I know."

"Must be true love, you out in this, trying to find her."

"No ma'am, just a girl. Like my sister."

"Well, you might as well go on back to Austin. You ain't going to find her in this. All you going to do is get yourself killed or froze to death."

"What's the name of this place?"

"It's called Oneida. Oneida, Texas."

When his belly was full, he thought about what the woman had said. Maybe she was right. It would be near impossible to find anybody in this. He found his way back to the livery. It was the first warm night he had had in a while. He thought more about what the woman had said.

Somebody pulling one of the big doors open, woke him.

"Where'd you come from?"

"Rode in last night. Woman at the saloon said I could sleep here."

"No problem. You might have to muck out some stalls."

"Yes sir. I can do that."

The next day, the snow began to melt away and soon, you could see the street and water dripping from the building eaves.

"Well, I reckon that storm is over."

"Does it snow much around here?"

"Not like that. Might not see it again before January."

———————— ····· ————————

It was then that Donagon decided to go home and wait until spring to continue his tracking of the Comanche. He saddled up and rode out at sunup. He headed back toward the San Saba River and followed it downstream to the fork of Brady creek.

It was early December when he finally made it through the cold wintry winds and rounded a bend in the river. Ahead of him was the burned out cabin and still standing barn of the Steinke farm. His heart was heavy as he rode in and opened the gate to the corral and turned his horse loose. The only place for him to sleep out of the weather was in the barn.

He found a spot in the loft where there was still a stack of dried hay. He remembered times when he and Jenny had played together up there. Letting the memories flood his mind, he stood for a while and absorbed the feeling.

Looking out over the land from his perch, he saw a rider coming up the river. He sat and watched the lone rider until he recognized a face he had not seen in a while. Fred Fuller, one of the rangers who had served with him for a short time.

Donagon left his place in the loft and climbed down the ladder. When he walked out of the barn, the rider pulled up and seeing who he was rode on toward him.

"Donagon, that you?"

"It's me, Fuller. Where you headed?"

"Looking for you."

"What for?"

"No reason. Just checking to see what you are doing."

"What happened to the rangers?"

"I left, like you. Sarge got shot by one of them bank robbers a while back. Thought you might help me go and find them."

"What about the rangers? How come they don't go find them?"

"Governor asked me to do it. They made up a record for me, like I was a bank robber too."

"Why me?"

"Governor said they wouldn't suspect you since you already left the rangers."

"I got to stay here and build that cabin back for Jenny when she comes home."

"Help me catch them outlaws, I'll help you build that cabin."

Donagon thought about that for a while. "I'll have to sleep on it. Let you know tomorrow."

"Fair enough. Let's look at that cabin."

The two of them walked side by side across the yard to the cabin. There was not much left. They looked around for something they could use and found nothing.

"Looks like we better just start from scratch." Fuller commented.

"Yep. Jenny probably would be better off with a new place."

The next morning, Donagon spoke to Fuller with a determined serious look.

"I'll help you track them two. I think I've already seen them."

"Seen them? Where?"

"Place called Comanche Springs. Pretty sure one of them had a bank bag in his saddle bags."

"Why didn't you get them then?"

"Weren't no law man. I didn't know they had killed the sarge."

"You know where they was headed?"

"I think south. Probably to Mexico. Fred, I will help you look for them two til spring. Then I got to go look for Jenny."

"If we find them varmints, I'll help you build the cabin, and find Jenny!"

"We'll leave at first light."

———————— ….. ————————

They did not ride to the springs. Instead, they cut across and headed southwest toward the forks of the North Concho and the Middle Concho. That would make a shorter ride to the border. The young men were inexperienced in tracking outlaws and only knew they were probably going to Mexico. The history of Texas outlaws and training from their Sergeant told them that was the most likely place to look.

They were not recognized rangers, so they could cross the Rio Grande with no problem. It was a two-week ride to the border and they made it to Camp Eagle pass, a militia camp set up to stop illegal trade with Mexico.

Across the river was Piedras Negras, a wide open, town south of the border. American outlaws were welcomed with open arms because of the money they usually brought with them.

The two young men rode across the river downstream of the town, so they could come in, not seen. They made their way to a shadowy alley and found the back door to one of the cantinas. Slipping inside, they sat at a table in the rear of a small dark room. There was two men at the bar wearing big sombreros and a lone woman seated at a table near the door.

After a while, one more man came in and joined the other two. No one seemed to be who they were looking for, so they slipped back into the alley and made their way to another cantina down the block. For several hours, they scoured the saloons in the border town with no success. Finally, they crossed back over the river and made camp on the Texas side.

"There are lots of towns along this river. You think we can make them all?" Fuller asked.

"I think we have to be patient."

"Not my long suit!"

"Why don't we get em to come to us? Set em up. We should be able to think of something. If you were a bank robber with lots of money, what would you be looking for?"

"Pretty girls! That's it! How do we do it?"

"First, we have to find them."

"I think we're close to where they are. I just feel it. This is the kind of town they would be in!" "I think you're right about that. Let's wait till tomorrow."

They fell asleep with a new resolve to find and arrest the outlaws.

For four days, they waited around cantinas, keeping an eye out for the robbers. They were just about to give up and go to another town when two men came riding across the border. It was two men, that Donagon had met before. Donagan and Fuller were walking down the street in broad daylight, and there was nowhere to avoid them. They were on the boardwalk when the two stepped down. One of them turned and then stopped in his tracks and turned back. "Don't I know you?"

"You look familiar too. Where did we meet?"

"You that young un was looking for them Comanche."

"That's right. Saw you at them springs."

"What you doing down here?"

"Same as you, I reckon. Looking for them pretty girls."

"Found any?'

"Not yet. We getting ready to go back across and see what's over there by that camp."

"Who's yore friend?"

"Fred, Fred Johnson. We met up in Oneida, right after I saw you."

"Well, we gonna see what's over here, then we'll go back. See you around."

"Don't wait too long. The soldier boys'll have all them girls. I think the best ones go over there to get them boys money."

"Well, we got a little bit of that to spread around. See you later."

Donagon and Fuller walked away and when the other two were out of sight went back to where they could watch them from an alley. For an hour, they followed them as they went in and out of cantinas. Finally, the one who had recognized Donagon threw his hands up as if they were arguing about something. He stomped away and mounted his horse, then looked back at his cohort, who mounted up and rode away with him. They rode back across the border. Waiting for half an hour, the two pursuers rode slowly across the narrow bridge into Texas. It wasn't long before they ran into the two outlaws again.

"Where ya'll been. We found the best girls in town. Just about had them talked into it when the law picked them up. Said we could have them back for fifty dollars bail each. Trouble is, we don't have fifty."

"How many is there?"

"Five, but we just need four."

"You sure they gonna let em out."

"That's what he said."

"Where they at?"

"Come on, we'll show you."

They walked down the boardwalk into the next block and across a dusty street. Donagon and Fuller opened a door and walked into the camp jail. One of the other two followed them, the other was suspicious and turned to walk away. Three of them walked into a room full of soldiers with weapons drawn. The other one was about to run when another soldier stepped in front of him.

"Going somewhere?"

"That's them. You'll find the money on their horses."

Chapter 9

But during the night an angel of the Lord opened the gates
of the prison, and taking them out, he said. Acts 5:19

For the next five years Donagon and Fuller spent
winters at the Steinke farm, and spring and summer
trying to find the renegade Comanche's who had
taken Jenny. They had ridden the Indian Nations from
one end to the other, following every lead they could
find. Hoping one would lead them to the band who
had taken the girl. It was becoming a futile effort.

On their last sojourn into the west side of the Oklahoma territory, they met a man who had spent many years with the Comanche. In their conversation, he remembered the young girl taken on the San Saba. His memory told him that she had been with the Comanche for two years and then sold to a white man who was going to take her to the mountains along the Rio Grande River.

Donagon and Fuller decided to check out what the man had said. They had exhausted just about every possible corner of the Nations and it was time to look somewhere else. It was late in the year and they would return to the farm and plan to begin their search on the Rio Grande in the spring.

When they got back to the San Saba in late November, they heard from a neighboring farmer the news that the United States of America was going to annex Texas as the twenty-eight state of the union. It came as no surprise, but they wondered what Mexico would do.

By the next spring as they were preparing to go search for Jenny in the Big Bend Mountains, Mexico began rumbling noises about taking Texas back. The Presidente was all for giving America that strip of land between the Nueces and the Rio rivers. The military deposed him and the war was on. Both of the former rangers felt obligated to fight for their Republic and once again became Texas rangers. Assigned to a company given the responsibility of patrolling the Nueces River.

There was more at stake than the battle with Mexico. Another threat was looming on the border of Mexico. Lipan Apache bands were making raids on both sides of the border. They used hit and run tactics and the Apache were very good at that kind of warfare.

The ranger company under the leadership of Captain Ely Stoddard chased the Apache every time they made a raid on a ranch or settlement along the river. It was hard to find their hiding places. They were very adept at hiding in the high country where they had the advantage.

Between chasing Mexicans back across the border and trying to find the Indians, the rangers were on patrol day and night. It was on a night patrol that Donagon and Fuller ran into a band of Lipan Apache. They, taken by surprise and before a shot was fired, were surrounded. There was nothing to do but let themselves become hostage. They were tied hand a foot and thrown across the back of their horses.

It was hard to see where they were going, but they both remembered crossing the river into Mexico. For four days, they rode across their saddles and found themselves climbing into a higher elevation. Once a day, one of the Indians would wet their lips from as water skin, just enough to keep them from dying.

One the fifth day they were led into a village well hidden in a small valley. A stream ran through the middle of the encampment and teepees lined on either side of it. The captives, thrown from their horses, left lying on the ground. When the sun went down, they were still lying there. Finally, a young woman came, gave them water, and untied their swollen hands. It was not much help. They still could not hold on to the skin to drink.

When the sun was coming over the mountains to the east, they were drug into a teepee and sat up. Two other women brought them flat bread and some kind of stew in a small crock. It did not smell very good, but both were too hungry to refuse it. They lost count of the days, and did not know how long, they were captives.

Somewhere in the night, they heard gunfire and sat up wondering what was happening. They knew the Apache did not have rifles. They only had bows and arrows. After a period, it became quiet again and they listened for voices. What they heard was the sound of muffled tones in a language they knew. It was Mexican.

An hour after the gunfire stopped, someone threw back the flap and peered into their tent.

Again, the Mexican voices began yelling to someone outside. Whomever they called came and looked at the two men and spoke to the other person. They wore the uniforms of the Mexican military.

It wasn't long before the two rangers were thrown back across their saddles and they felt themselves being led back down out of the high country.

_____ ….. _____

The next thing they knew, they was flung from their horses, carried into an adobe building, thrown into what appeared to be a cell. It was cold, damp and dark. They tried to sleep, but the cold, wet ground kept them awake. Sunshine streaked through a tiny window, but not enough to warm their bodies. At least they could see enough to figure out they were in a jail cell. There was no one else there with them. It seemed like hours before they heard a movement outside and the clanging of keys in a lock.

Two men dressed in the same uniform came into the cell and stood above them speaking in their native tongue. They only stayed a few minutes, then left, locking the cell behind them. Finally, the clanging of keys again brought them a bucket of water and two flour tortillas. It was not enough to satisfy their hunger, but they devoured them and drank all the water.

Fuller tried to speak, but his throat was dry and cracked, and his words came out in a whisper.

"Where do you think we are?"

"I know we're somewhere in Mexico. Probably prisoners of war. Could get shot." His voice too was only a whisper. "Better start looking for a way out of here."

It was hard to see in the dark cell, but both men began to squint and look for any signs of a weakness in the walls and the tiny window. Donagon began to chip away at a crack in the wall just below the window.

After what seemed like a week of water and flour tortillas, and slow chipping at the wall, the cell opened and another body fell into the cell with them. It was hard to tell in the dark who it was.

"Are you Americans?" A voice stronger than theirs asked.

"Yes." Donagon whispered.

"So am. They took me on the border. I am part of the seventh Calvary. Was patrolling along the river and a bunch of Juaristas came across and captured me.

"Why are you not wearing a uniform?"

"I am a civilian scout."

It was too taxing on their voices so they did not talk anymore. Donagon chipped away at the wall for another day and finally saw a slim streak of light show through.

He stopped and showed it to the others

"Better wait til dark to do any more." He sat with his back against the crack.

Dinner arrived and they saved a small amount of water to soften the mud wall. As soon as the light streak disappeared from the window, they all began to work on the wall. Sometime before daylight, the hole was large enough for one of them to slip through. One at a time, they all slithered through the opening and made it outside the cell. A dog barked in the distance, and they knew they had to get as far away from the building as they could before daybreak.

In a moonless night, they could see what looked to be trees on the horizon so they stealthily headed in that direction. Moving into the trees, made it harder to see where they were going. They only knew they must wait until it was light.

After what seemed like hours of stumbling over roots and falling onto hard ground, they came out of the woods and found themselves on the bank of a narrow stream. All three men slipped full body into the cool water and soaked it into their dry, starving bodies. They drank their fill and just laid and let it soak in.

They waited for the sun to tell them what was north and which way to go to the Rio Grande. As soon as it peeked over the horizon, they left the water and headed out. Moving as swiftly as they could on rough ground and barefoot, they headed for Texas.

There was little population and they only saw an occasional thatched roof hut. They avoided contact with people. Traveling in the daytime and finding a place to sleep at night, took them more than a week to make their way to the border. They're only source of food was what they could steal from the peons along the way, and that wasn't much.

When they crossed the river, their new traveling companion was near to his post at Camp Eagle Pass.

"I reckon you can check in with my commander. I don't know where the rangers are now."

"We never got your name." Donagon was curious.

"I am Captain Robert E. Lee. I am in the command of General Winfield Scott."

"Well, thank you captain. I reckon we'll go on back to the Nueces and find our company. We will go with you to get some food, though."

They had crossed over the border somewhere downstream of the camp and had to walk another half day to get there.

"Captain, you ever hear of a white man on them mountains up yonder with a young white girl?" He pointed to the white peaks of Big Bend.

"Saw a man one time headed up there. He was trying to hide a child about twelve. Wouldn't let me get close enough to see if it was a boy or girl."

_____ ….. _____

Parting company with the captain, they struck out north to rejoin their ranger company. Captain Lee had managed to wrangle a couple of horses for them. Three days later, they were back with their company and fighting the Apache once more. Donagon kept in the back of his mind what Lee had said. When this war was over, he would search those mountains for Jenny.

It was almost another year before the Mexicans were defeated. It was turning winter everywhere else, but south Texas never felt the cold of harsh winters. Except for the peaks of Big Bend.

Donagon and his partner, Fred Fuller, decided to take one stab at the mountains before heading north to the San Saba. They found pack animals and set out for the cold, mountaintops. Surely if Jenny were there, they would find her. Riding in the upper elevation was hard on two men who had never traversed the high country before. They searched until the snow levels were impossible to maneuver in, then gave it up.

They struggled in the deep drifts and spent many cold nights curled up in Buffalo robes they had traded for with a band of Tonkawa Indians.

One of the especially cold stormy day, they found a small cabin built into the side of a sharp cliff. It was their first night out of the freezing weather. They were able to gather enough wood for a fire and for the first time got their bodies warm. They found that someone had kept a stock of smoked fish and game in the cabin. It looked as if someone had been living there, and were just gone for a while. Making themselves at home, they ate their fill of the food, and tried to replace as much as they could.

"Wonder where the man is owns this cabin?"

"Must be out running traps, or off looking for more game. Don't guess he'll mind we stay to warm up."

They stayed in the cabin for four days trying to thaw themselves.

Fred Fuller vowed to himself, he would never be that cold again. The weather was not clearing by the fourth day, so they made the decision to get down off those mountains as quick as they could.

It was another week of nearly freezing to death before they found the air was getting warmer and the snow shallower. When they found flat land again, they headed for the San Saba River.

Chapter 10

For they are My servants whom I bought out from the land
of Egypt: they are not to be sold in a slave sale. Leviticus 25:42

The farm looked like it never had before. Both of
them, without speaking of it, were content to spend a
winter working the land. Donagon kept thinking about
Jenny and how she was holding up if she were in
those cold mountains.

The two of them kept busy with planting. The winter months were for cultivating and getting the ground ready. In early spring, they planted one acre of cotton for a cash crop, ten acres of corn for corn and meal, one acre of sorghum for sugar, and a small garden in the plot that Mary Steinke had used for her vegetables.

This year a German couple had stopped by in search of farmland and Donagon was more than happy to let them stay on the farm and work on shares for a place over their head. He knew they would leave when they found a place of their own, but for now they were a welcome addition to the Steinke farm.

It was a cold rainy winter on the San Saba. The couple from Germany turned out to be a truly hard working family. Heinz and Sophia Schroder were just happy to have a roof over their head. She was with child and they were glad it would be born in America. Donagon and Fuller kept an eye out for signs of hostile Indians. Several years had passed, since the raid that took the life of the Steinke's, The Texas rangers were very effective, keeping them at bay.

When the Mexican war was over, Donagon and Fuller once more left the service to continue the search for Jenny. This year, they would go in a different direction. They would go back to the Big Bend Mountains and see what they looked like with no snow falling. Fuller was anxious about leaving too early and Donagon wanted to get an early start. There was nothing said between them, but it was obvious they disagreed. Fuller had gotten irritable in the last weeks and when Donagon was ready to go, refused to ride with him.

"I will meet you at Comanche Springs later." He told his friend.

"Suit yourself. I am leaving now." He waved to Fuller and the Schroders as he rode away from the farm.

There was still a late chill in the air as he rode along the riverbank. He looked at an ominous sky and hoped it would not be a late storm. He was wrong. By day's end, he was wearing a poncho and fighting against a blowing wind and rain. He stopped early and camped near the riverbank under a group of Cedar trees. The water was rising fast and almost out of the banks by the time, it was dark.

Donagon looked around for another group of trees to move under and saw a faint glimmer of light in the distance. Someone had a fire going some fifty yards away from his position, and back away from the rising water. Using the fire as a guide, he led his horse in that direction, fighting against the rain. When he was close enough to make out a form through the pouring rain, he saw two people sitting under the tree covered with a poncho. He could not tell who or what they were. He yelled as loud as he could against the blowing rain.

"Hello, the camp."

No one heard him so he yelled louder.

"Hello, the camp. I'm coming in!"

Still, no one heard him so he walked slowly toward the two sitting figures. When he was almost upon the fire, one of the men heard someone coming through the rain, and reached to his side and pulled a revolver.

"Whoever you are, come in slow."

"I'm coming in now. My hands are raised."Donagon could hardly see through the water dripping off the brim of his hat. He eased through the rain and came as close to the fire as he dared.

"River's rising. Had to move away from the water. Saw your fire. That coffee I smell?"

"Pour yourself a cup, stranger. Don't spect much company fore this rain quits."

Donagon got a cup from his saddlebags and poured a cup of the hot coffee. Near the boiling point, it would remove the chill in his bones. Three men sat around a fire under Cedar trees and drank without speaking. Soon, all three of them were fast asleep under their ponchos. Sometime in the night, the rain stopped, but none of them woke.

Birds singing in the trees woke Donagon and one of the men was scrounging around for dry sticks. The fire had burned down while they slept.

"Don't look like we gonna have a fire today."

"I reckon not."

"Who you be, mister?"

"Name is Donagon. How about you boys?"

"I'm Bob Murphy. That yonder is my brother Danny. Say! Ain't you that feller what's looking for that girl took by them Comanch?"

"That's me. You heard anything?"

"Heard she was living over by Oneida with a half breed."

"Where over by Oneida?"

"Heard they was in a shack between that Palo Dura canyon and the town. Folks is laughing cause you running all over the Nations and she be right here."

"Thank's, Bob. I'll go see for myself."

"Good luck, mister. " He was still chuckling and waving his head as Donagon saddled and rode off. It was a long shot, but he had to check out every lead about Jenny's whereabouts. The sky had turned a bright blue and the rain had washed everything clean.

This time when he rode along the edge of Palo Dura, it was a spring morning instead of in a blizzard. The whole countryside was abloom in yellow flowers. The hard rain the day before had shot them up and the plain was a waving sheet of yellow.

About mid-day, he spotted an adobe cabin off to his left. He pulled rein and turned to go see if Jenny was there. When he drew near, he saw a lone woman standing with one hand shading her eyes against the bright sun. She had long blond hair.

He stopped and sat staring at her for a long minute, then rode on in.

"Morning, ma'am. Would you mind telling me your name?"

"Well, it sure enough ain't Jenny. You that feller looking for her?"

"Yes ma'am. I'm Dave Donagon."

"Sure do hope you find that girl, mister. Everybody comes by here wants me to be Jenny. You offering some kind of reward?"

"No ma'am. Just trying to find a friend took by the Comanche."

"How long they had her now?"

"Little over eight years now."

"Don't you think it's about time to give up? She's probably dead or wife to one of them Comanche by now."

"I'll just keep looking. So long ma'am. Thanks for your time."

_____ ….. _____

That woman may have been telling him the truth.
Sometimes he wondered if he should give it up.
Something inside of him would not let him do that. He
would find Jenny, either a marker on her grave, or the
red or white man who had taken her for a wife. He
had to know, and he would not stop looking until he
did. He had wasted nearly a week turning north to go
by that woman's cabin. Now he had to get to the
valley and see if Fuller was there waiting for him.
Turning back south, he headed for Comanche Springs
where he would rest and wait for Fred Fuller. It was a
long ride and he did not want to miss meeting his
friend. He stepped up the pace and rode longer days.
The days seemed longer and he had been riding with
Fuller so long, he missed the comradery.

He had spent the night on Yellow house draw and
was packing his gear away when he saw a movement
out of the corner of his eye. Since his encounter with
the Apache, Donagon had gotten weary of someone
slipping up on him. He had forgotten how wily the
Comanche could be. He reached for his Henry
repeater, but before he reached it, one of them raised a
tomahawk into the air.

The Indian stopped when he saw the scar on
Donagon's head. He grunted and said something to
the other one and pointed to Donagon's head. They
threw him on the ground and tied his hands behind
him with rawhide. Once again, he was a captive of
hostiles. This time his mind was set on the possibility
of finding Jenny among his captors.

They threw him over the back of his horse and
yelping and pointing, rode off with one in front and
three behind their hostage. For three days, they let him

go without food or water. They had not even taken him off the horse.

Finally, one of them lifted his head and poured water into his mouth, nearly choking him. That night they threw him violently to the ground and tossed a flour tortilla near his face. His hands still tied, he had to find it with his mouth and draw it in, dirt and all.

They continued riding until they were at the springs, and a rendezvous with a larger group of their own tribe. Donagon was familiar with the Comanche trade meets. He knew, even in his state of mind, there would be hostages there. He was drug off the animal and into one of the teepees and left tied.

At some point, a woman came into the teepee and untied his hands. She sat a bowl with some sort of broth and a flour tortilla next to him and then left. His hands were numb and stiff from the rawhide and he had to spend a long time trying to rub circulation back into them. He finally had enough feeling to hold the bowl close to his mouth and sip the warm liquid. He finished the food, and then fell back and went into a deep sleep.

The Comanche came and drug him out after four days. It was trade day, and the springs had filled up with many more teepees and some white people looking for their family members. He squinted against the sun and tried to see the other hostages, as he was being drug to a spot near them. If Jenny were there, he would surely be able to recognize her.

All day there was bantering and yelling among the Comanche and other tribes who were trying to get their people back. Each time a woman put up for bids, Donagon tried to see if it was Jenny. He had not seen anyone who looked like her, but then, it had been eight years.

For days, they drug him back and forth to watch the ceremonies. Their families purchased some of the white eyes back and quickly left. Those who had no one to save him or her, sold to the highest bidder. Some as wives to Mexicans or white trappers, and some as slaves to the Mexican silver mines.

Donagon, along with three others, was the last sold into slavery at one of the mines. He was loaded onto a wagon with the three other men. None of them was white men. Two were Tonkawa Indians and one was a Mexican breed. All four of them, trussed up like cargo, laid side by side in the wagon, and driven towards the border. After five days of hot, dry baking in the sun, they arrived at the river. All were drug from the wagon and thrown into the water.

As badly burned as they were, it felt good to soak in the cool flowing waters of the Rio Grande. They had their hands loosened and fed a bowl of cold beans and flat bread. None of them spoke. Partly, because they couldn't talk through parched lips, and partly because they would not have understood the other's language.

They were loaded back into the wagons after only thirty minutes and began another long, hot, ride. It was a long grueling ride to the silver mines deep in the mountains of south Mexico. Two weeks after they left the border, they arrived at an encampment of adobe shacks. They were once more drug from the wagon and thrown onto a damp surface in one of the huts. Thrown hard onto a dirt floor, they heard a door lock behind them.

For the next four days, they ate much better than they had on the trail. A woman brought them warm beans and tortillas three times a day. It was so they would regain their strength and be strong enough to work the mines.

On the fifth day, forced into a line with thirty or forty more men who looked like zombies, they made their daily trek into the mines.

Donagon began looking around for a means of escape. There were guards all around the walking dead and on the sides of the hills surrounding the mines. All were heavily armed. It would not be an easy thing to do, but he knew he had to get away and go back on the quest for Jenny. That thought would keep him going.

Chapter 11

It was for freedom that Christ set us free: therefore keep
standing firm and do not be subject again to a yoke of slavery.
Galatians 5:1

Fred Fuller pulled out of the Steinke farm headed
south to go meet Donagon at Comanche Springs. He
had no idea what had happened to his partner. For
some reason, he did not like the snow or cold weather
in the Big Bend Mountains. Never before had he been
afraid of anything, but dying in the cold scared him.
He rode slow, mulling things over in his mind. He was
sure he would be at the springs before Donagon.

Several times, he had seen Indians riding along his trail, but off in the distance. None of them had come close enough for him to see what tribe they were. Keeping an eye out, he rode under whatever cover he could find, which was not much in the Texas southwest. When he stopped for the night, he hobbled his horse close by because he was afraid a hostile would take it.

He awoke early, saddled his mount, started out of camp and found a band of Comanche was following him. It was either fight or run and he chose to run. He kicked his horse and took off at a gallop, Indians in hot pursuit. Nearing the Colorado River, he looked for a place for cover so he could make a stand. What he saw ahead of him was a wall of painted rock. There were Indian symbols painted on every surface.

Realizing he was in their territory, he had no choice but to get to a high place and try to pick off as many as he could before they got him. *This time, he would not, be taken alive.* Finding a crevice in a rock formation, he pulled his Henry from the boot and began rapid firing at the redskins. For an hour, they tried to get to his position, but he held them off.

Suddenly he saw out of the corner of his eye a movement in the rocks above him. A shadow fell on the wall in front of him and he knew his time was running out. They had him surrounded and were beginning to move in.

Just when he thought it was over, a shot rang out somewhere in the hills behind him. One of the shadows toppled from above him and fell to their death below. Someone had come to his aid. Another round of rapid fire and another Indian fell from his vantage point. When he turned to look back down, he saw the remainder of the Comanche mounting their bareback animals and riding away.

Fuller had no idea who have protected his hide, but someone did. He stood and looked around, waiting for his savior to show himself. Finally, a lone figure stepped out of the rocks and waved to him. He pointed toward the river and Fuller climbed down and walked to the bank of the Colorado.

He came out of a clump of mesquite in time to see another man standing by the river.

"Reckon them Comanch had enough. Looked like they wanted yore scalp."

"Reckon they'd had it, you hadn't come along when you did."

"I spect so. Name is Barnes. Roscoe's my front name. What's yourn?"

"Fred Fuller. Glad to meet you Roscoe."

"Fuller? Ain't you one of them fellers been looking fer that gal got took by them Comanch?"

"Yes sir. Have you seen her?"

"Nope. Just heard yore name somewhere. Where's yore partner?"

"I was going to meet him at Comanche Springs. Reckon I still will."

"Ain't there! I was there more'n a week ago. I think yore partner was sold to them Mex miners."

"You think he was?" You don't know for sure?"

"I'm purty sure that was him. Him, and three others sold together. Them Mex's will work them til they're dead and go get some more to take their place."

"You know where in Mexico?"

"Nope. Just heard it was a long way from here. Ain't no need in you going lookin for him. Them Mex's kill you too."

"Know anybody who does know where the mines are?"

"Nope. Well one man might. I think he was down there one time. Not sure he's even still alive. Name is Carl Webster. Last thing I heard he was married to one of them Mex senoritas. Lived down in Durango. Ain't no guarantee he'll help you if he does know."

"I reckon I'll have to go and see. Any chance Donagon is still alive, I have to help him. Guess I will be going down to Durango. Thanks for your help, mister."

Fuller waited until the following morning before heading down to the Rio Grande and across into Mexico. It was another week of riding and he was not even sure of where to cross the river. He would just head in that direction and find his way once in Mexico.

_____ ….. _____

The river was up and running wild from the spring snow melting in the San Juan Mountains of Colorado. It was nearly out of the banks and Fuller had to ride up and down looking for a place to cross. He finally found a narrow, shallow spot downstream, and eased into the cold, rushing water.

After twenty minutes of slow moving, he made it to the other bank. He was now in Mexico and subject to their laws.

Fuller was unsure of which direction to go so he stopped in the first Colonia he came to. When he rode in everyone seemed to disappear into thatched roof, adobe huts. He rode through the one short dirt path and then turned and rode back through. Finally, an older man stepped out and stood with his sombrero in his hand.

"Senor?"

¿«Vous connaissez le moyen de Durango?» He asked for direction to Durango.

"Si, señor ir por ese camino". The old man pointed to the southwest.

"Gracias, señor. ¿Tienes cualquier agua?" He thanked the old peon and asked for a drink of water.

"No, señor. No tenemos agua."

The old one seemed disturbed by his request and told him no. Something had spooked these people, and they were afraid to speak to strangers. Fuller pulled his horses head around and rode to where Durango lied.

The country was dry and hot, like riding through a desert. He would have to ride slow and preserve his water. For three days, he rode through the arid land without seeing a single soul. He was beginning to think the old man had sent in the wrong way. Nearly asleep in the saddle, he rode along at the pace of his horse. Sometime in the late afternoon, he spied a Colonia rising out of the land like a mirage. Heat was steaming off the scorching, rocky, caliche.

He rode slowly into the small village and saw several men dressed in sparkling white clothing. They all wore large wide brimmed sombreros.

"Hola. Podría indicarme el camino a Durango?" Once again, he asked the way to Durango. Once again, the peon pointed to the southwest. *Maybe the old man had told him right.*

He stepped down and walked to a round vessel that held water. He dipped his canteen and filled it full. When he turned, there were several women and small children watching him. One of the women was holding a bowl of hot frijoles. Another one, flour tortillas. They were friendlier than the first place he had been. He sat on a tree stump and ate the food, while the kids watched curiously.

No one spoke another word, and when Fuller finished he said gracious, and mounted his horse and rode out. He had no idea whether he would find Donagon dead or alive or find him at all, but he felt it his duty to try to find his partner. He rode on in the sweltering heat for another five days and found himself climbing into a higher elevation.

He was in the Sierra del Tlahualilo Mountains. It was not a high range like Big Bend, and he saw no snow covered peaks. He would climb for two days and then start a descent down the other side. It was cool up there but not so he was afraid.

He was getting near to Durango and the silver mines the man told him about. Soon, he would know if Donagon was dead or alive. When he came down from the mountains, he found a well-traveled wagon road leading to the larger town of Durango.

_____ ..... _____

He stopped and found a place in the shade under a tree and waited until the sun was beginning to go down in the west. He thought it better to go in under the cover of darkness. That way he could nose around and find out more about the mining operation. Just at dark, he saw lanterns being lit and hung outside doors and on dilapidated overhangs. The sound of a mariachi band started the evening for the one cantina.

Laughter filled the air as the men of the town filtered in and began their daily intake of tequila. Most of them were guards for the silver mines. Fuller knew that he would stick out like a sore thumb if he was seen as a foreign gringo.

He hid in the shadows, and watched and waited as the locals came and went. When one of them left the cantina alone, he followed. Keeping in the shadows close to walls, ducking into alleys until he was at the end of a street, out of the light. He slipped up behind the Mexican and with one quick move, slammed a revolver onto the back of his head. Dragging him into an alley, he removed the white garments and sombrero.

Leaving the man lie, he took the clothes and made his way back to where he had left his horse. Riding out of town, he found a grove of mesquite and changed into the frock of a Mexican peon. Leaving his horse hobbled in the trees, he made his way back into Durango and sat on a bench near the cantina.

No one noticed another drunk peon, and he was able to overhear conversations. His Spanish was limited, but good enough to get an idea what they were saying. He heard nothing about mining or the gringos. The only way he would find what he needed was to follow some of the guards. They were easy to spot by the clothes they wore. All of them were dressed in a uniform with matching narrow brimmed sombreros.

Two of them left the cantina, and staggered out to the edge of town and turned down a winding side road that led to a group of buildings in a circular cluster. Even in the dark, Fuller could see the entrance to a mineshaft. It was nestled in a group of large boulders. Lanterns hung in a makeshift fashion above the path from the buildings to the shaft.

Under the light, he could see all the buildings locked, from the outside. There was no way to know if Donagon was in one unless he found a hiding place to watch. While it was still dark, he searched around and found a perch in the rocks that gave him a view of the buildings.

Leaning back against the boulder, he slept until the sun was peeking over the horizon. When he woke, he heard voices below and looked to see guards unlocking each heavy door. Men filed out of each stockade in single file and marched to a common area where they sat at tables and were fed a sparse breakfast. It was hard to tell if Donagon was one of them. They were all dressed alike, and all were frail from lack of food Fuller strained to look into each face and it was still hard to tell.

He would somehow have to get closer. Searching from his hiding place, he saw that he would have to get down on their level. That would be hard without someone seeing him. Knowing that he could not risk getting caught, or both he and Donagon would die in this place, he eased down behind the boulders and slowly inched his way around to get a closer look.

Finding he could get within twenty feet and no nearer, he settled in to wait and watch until the slaves were marched from breakfast to the mine. It wasn't long before the guards began yelling at them to move. Fuller stared into the face of each man as he walked by. After thirty ragged slaves went by, he looked into a face that he recognized, even in the state he was in. Donagon was indeed one of the slaves and alive. Now all he had to do was figure out a way to set his friend free.

It would have to be some kind of commotion. He knew he would have to create a distraction. First, he would have to find some way to let Donagon know he was there. That would take some thinking and finesse. Thinking about it while he watched the others March to their work place, he saw a way. Across the way, near the shaft entrance was a box with the Spanish word for dynamite, explosivo.

He made his way to the box, by slipping around boulders and inching his way along, watching every move the guards made. When the slaves were all in the shaft, all but three of the guards went back to the dining area to smoke and drink coffee. Fuller managed to slip close enough to one of the boxes to reach in and remove four sticks of explosives. In another box, he found caps and fuse.

Quickly, he returned to his perch and waited for the day to end and the slaves returned to their cells. His plan was to blow part of one of the boulders down onto the walk path the guards took the prisoners on to get them back to their beds. Fuller slept until an hour before the mine shut down for the day, then waited for them to come out. It was near dark, when the three guards who had spent the day guarding the workers, brought them out.

He timed the fuse so he would just have time to jump down before the explosion threw part of the boulder onto the guards. He planned for the dust from the blast to be his cover. Lighting the fuse, he then counted to ten and jumped just as the boulder showered the slaves with dirt and rock. He had already picked Donagon out of the crowd, and grabbed him by the arm and ran behind a building. The guards who were drinking coffee came running, but Fuller and Donagon were already away from them. It would take hours for them to get a head count.

Chapter 12

Is this not the fast which I choose, To loosen the bonds of wickedness, To undo the bands of the yoke, And to let the oppressed go free And break every yoke. Isaiah 58: 6

"Where did you come from?"

"Somewhere along the San Saba. You alright?"

"I will be. Let's get out of here! You bring me a horse?"

"You asking a lot for somebody been on vacation down here. Reckon you'll have to ride double til we find one."

"Where did you get them clothes? You look like some kind of Mexican peon."

"Look better'n you."

"I reckon. Sure good to see your ugly face. Wait! We need to see if we can help one of those other men."

"We can't go back in there! Both of us will die there."

"That half breed! He saved my life. I owe him!" Donagon turned and looked back at the turmoil Fuller had created. Dust still filled the air. The guards were rounding up the slaves and herding them into the feeding area. The one Donagon owed his life to, was standing near the edge of the tables rubbing dirt from his eyes and wondering what had come about. No one but Donagon knew what had happened.

Before Fuller could stop him, Donagon had slipped along a wall just outside the lantern light and was standing behind his friend. With tears from the dust, streaming down his face Juan Carlos O'Hare could see that it was Donagon.

"Come on. Let's get out of here!" He led O'Hare to the back of the building where Fuller waited. "Nobody saw us. We better git!"

They wormed their way through the darkness of back alleys and out the other side of Durango. There were guards walking the streets of Durango looking for someone. They only knew there was an explosion of some kind. They did not know who or what had caused it.

Fuller's horse was right where he had left it.

"How do you propose we ride out of here?"

"No, senor. I will walk."

"You better walk fast. Don't want them guards to catch you." Fuller swung a leg over and held his hand out for Donagon. Juan Carlos O'Hare was already gone. They headed into the mountains, and looked for a place to stop and gather themselves. A small light caught their eye as the rounded a large boulder.

Fuller pulled rein and squinted into the darkness trying to see what it was. He realized it was a fire. A small fire made with dry sticks that created no smoke. Donagon peered around him and saw the flame too.

"Juan."

Fuller looked at him, and then rode on in. It was O'Hare, who had been there ahead of them long enough to build a fire. They got down and walked to the fire ring.

"Coffee would be nice. Ain't had a cup in a while."

"I think I can do that." Fuller reached into his saddlebags and retrieved a blue porcelain pot and a canvas bag with coffee.

"I guess you want some frijoles, too?"

"No, we had plenty of them back there. You got any fatback?"

Fred got a fry pan, and cut long strips of fatback and threw them in.

"We better take turns on watch. Those folks ain't going to like you taking off like that."

"I spect you right. I'll take first watch."

"No. You and the breed need to sleep. I'll take first turn."

"Careful about calling him a breed. He thinks he's Irish."

"Irish? With a name like Juan Garcia?"

"Juan Garcia O'Hare."

"Don't bother me none, he wants to be Irish. I'll kiss the blarney stone. Now, you better get some sleep."

At first light, O'Hare was on watch and already had a pot of coffee brewing when the other two woke up.

"Blimey, mates! I thought you was going to sleep all day."

Fuller looked at Donagon. "Didn't I hear him calling me Senor, last night? Sounded like a Mex, then."

"He can sound like whatever he wishes. I spect it will come in handy. He can even speak Comanche."

"How'd he learn that?"

"Spent twenty years with em. Been all over the country with them red devils. Knows everywhere they been."

"That's why you brung him along."

"Nope! He really did save my life. I was sold with three other men. Two were Tonkawa, but the other was a Mexican breed. Part Comanche, I think. He made a knife out of a piece of flint. Had it hid in his pants. Tried to steal my food. I didn't see the knife but O'Hare did. Shoved it all the way in the breed. Like I said, I owe him my life."

"That and he might lead us to Jenny."

"That too."

_____ ….. _____

For the next week, they rode and walked across the desert of Mexico. O'Hare was able to keep up with the other two, even though he was on foot. They managed to find water and food at some of the small Colonia's along the way.

The Irish Mexican was adept at finding food where they least expected it. He could be Irish one minute and the next, talking to the peons in their language. He had learned to be a scavenger on the streets of Dublin as a young boy. How he got the names of Juan Garcia, he did not say.

Somewhere along their trail, he came back riding a horse and leading another. Neither had saddles and looked like both had seen their last days. The closer they got to the border, the more people they saw. It would have been better to ride at night, but they did not know the land.

Late in a long day, they stopped to take a drink of water. O'Hare perked his ears

"Listen."

Donagon and Fuller looked at each other. There was a faint noise coming from somewhere. It sounded familiar but out of place. They rode on until the sound became clearer. It was a mariachi band.

Just at dusk, they rode in to the border town of Piedras Negras. They were one river crossing away from being back in Texas. Both Donagon and Fuller had been here before. They were Texas rangers then. They wondered if Robert E. Lee was still there.

_____ ….. _____

During the long hot days in the mine, Donagon had gotten to know O'Hare well. His father had traveled to Spain and found a Spanish wife. He brought her back to Dublin and started a family. Juan Garcia, named after his mother's father. When the boy was only six, they had come to America to escape the rebellion.

In their first days in Texas, a Comanche war party killed Maria O'Hare and her husband. The boy was then taken hostage and raised as a Comanche brave.

O'Hare unlike Donagon, was not sold by the Comanche, but taken by the mine slavers, while helping to load slaves onto a wagon. Managing to keep his Irish tongue, he was also fluent in Spanish and Comanche.

Donagon also knew that he could help them to find the Comanche strongholds and possibly Jenny Steinke. Once more, he was on the trail of a young girl who by now would be a woman. Sometimes he felt the search useless, but he could not give up until he had found her, dead or alive.

_____ ….. _____

O'Hare had been with the Comanche for a long time, and had even been on war parties with them. He had seen captives come and go, but did not remember the girl that Donagon had told him about. It had to be another band of Comanche that had taken her.

What he did know, was where the Comanche had all their meeting places. There were many of them in Mexico. It was almost a game to the Indians to cross the border and raid Mexican ranches and farms. He had been on some of those raids too.

He and Donagon had become friends since that Mex had tried to stab Donagon. He was obligated to help his friend find the girl, if he could.

"Where do you think we ought to look first?"

"You said she might be in the Big Bend. I reckon we can go there. They rendezvous in a couple of other places between here and there. Guess we could look at them first.

"You lead the way."

"Soon as I find me a horse."

Donagon had not thought about O'Hare walking all the way from the mines in Durango.

"Where do you plan on doing that?"

"I am Comanche. I know how to find horse!" He disappeared for an hour. When he returned he was on a horse.

They began a ride up the Rio Grande River. Two days later, they found an encampment at San Carlos on the Mexican side of the river. There was a small band of Comanche there, but no hostages. Juan had gone in while the other two waited for him across the river. He slipped back in after dark.

"She is not in there. They have no captives with them."

"Where do we go from here?"

"I think we should stop at the Tonkawa village. It is up the river about four days from here. They do not take hostages, but they may know who the Comanche have. From there it is only about another week into the Big Bend Mountains."

"Okay. We leave at daylight."

They stayed on the Texas side of the river for their ride to the Tonkawa village. For four days, they rode near the river and kept an eye out for signs of Comanche. Late on the last day, they saw the glow of flames in a circle near the bank of the river.It was just about sundown when they rode into the village. A group of friendly people greeted them as they rode in.

Seated in front of a teepee, they spoke to a chief called Brown beaver and fed by the women. The chief spoke long into the night, and they were finally, given a place to sleep in a teepee. It was the first time two of them had slept indoors since the stockade at the mine.

After a good night of rest, they put their coffee pot over the flames of one of the cook fires. The Tonkawa allowed it, but refused to drink the smelly white man brew. The chief was in a talkative mood when he came out. He told them of the times the Tonkawa had spent on a creek bank with healing waters.

The Tonkawa yearned to go back to the fertile banks of Salado creek. It was a happy time for them. That was before hostile tribes had chased them from their home. That and a heavy influx of white men settling the land around them. The white men had begun to drive cattle over their land and build bridges to cross over the creek. An outbreak of fever had killed many of his people and many more had died on the trail to this part of Texas.

The land in south Texas and Mexico was not green and fertile as it had been where they left. The chief rambled on and on and soon, he was joined by other men of his tribe. It became a session of mourning and pain for their homeland.

Donagon, Fuller, and O'Hare sat respectively and listened to the chants of the Tonkawa people. Soon, the women were bringing them more food to eat. After that an afternoon of the same lament. It was as though the Tonkawa had been waiting for someone to hear their tale of woe. By the time, they had settled down, it was near dark again. They would stay another night with their new friends.

Chapter 13

Then the Lord knows how to rescue the godly from
temptation, and to keep the unrighteous under punishment for the
day of judgment. 2 peter 2:9

They turned west and headed into the big bend
mountains. The last they had heard, Jenny sold to a
white man who was a trapper in the mountains along
the Rio Grande. Fuller was okay about going into the
high elevations when it was not cold and snowing.

All summer long, they searched the mountains for a trapper and a young woman. On more than one occasion, one of them thought they had seen a woman running silently through the trees, but each time whatever it was disappeared like a ghost. It was a frustrating time for Donagon who was beginning to lose hope of ever finding her.

 O'Hare had told them of a place west of the mountains, near Presidio. It was one of the many places, the Comanche wintered. He had seen several young white women in his years with the Indians, but did not remember the one they searched for. It was a last resort for the searchers. Donagon and Fuller had just about looked in every corner of the state and most of the Indian nations without any sign of the girl.

By the time they reached Presidio, the days were beginning to get shorter and even that far south there was a change in the weather. Crossing over the border, they spent another month searching for Jenny. O'Hare led them to four different places that the Comanche had wintered in Mexico. It was to early for the tribe to be moving south of the border, and most had been relocated to the Oklahoma territory. It was time to head back to the San Saba, before the mountains of Big Bend became impassable.

Once again,`Donagon was heading back to the Steinke homestead without bringing Jenny with him. Another year had passed without any success. He was nearing his twenty-fifth year and knew that Jenny would now be twenty- two. He was no longer looking for a girl child, but a woman.

The three riders crossed back over the river and headed into the high country once again. Fred Fuller was not looking forward to crossing the high peaks again. He was still not comfortable with the long, cold winter storms. O'Hare was not much different. He too, was frightened of getting stranded and dying in one of the deep snow banks.

When they started up into the high ground, it began to snow heavily.

"We need to find a place to get out of this." Fred was getting nervous.

"Should be a couple of days to that cabin we stayed in before. We should make that okay. We can wait it out there!" Donagon ,to be heard, had to raise his voice, over the increasing winds.

O'Hare yelled above the wind. "I don't like this. I think I'll go back down to Presidio!"

"I think I will go with you!" Fuller looked at Donagon.

"I'm going on!" Donagon looked at his two friends. He knew that Fuller was afraid of snowstorms. "See you at San Saba!"
Fuller and O'Hare sat and watched Donagon until he was out of sight in the blowing snow. They turned and rode back down out of the snowcapped mountains to the flat lands and warmth. Fred stopped and looked back over his shoulder, hoping his partner would be okay.

_____ ..... _____

The wind and snow was getting much harder and louder as Donagon made his way upward. The temperature was dropping and it was getting difficult for the lone rider to see. He kept plodding along, his horse stumbling in the deep, white powder. He was beginning to wish he had gone back down with his friends. Finally, it was snowing too hard for him to see where he was going. He dismounted and led his horse through the deepening drifts. It was so over cast, he could not tell whether it was still day or night.

His eyes were beginning to cloud over and his eyebrows were frozen. He could no longer see where he was going. Donagon was sure he had made a mistake by not going back down with the others. They would sleep in a warm place and he was going to freeze to death in a snowstorm. Stepping on a tree root, he stumbled and fell.

It felt good to lie down, so he just thought he would rest for a minute. Closing his eyes against the freezing cold, he began to drift off. He could see Fuller and O'Hare seated by a warm fire eating frijoles and drinking hot coffee. *Hot coffee. That was it!* He needed to build a fire and make a pot of coffee. He scratched around in the snow for firewood and could not come up with anything.

Sleep overcame him and he could not fight it back. He tried to keep talking aloud and even began to yell into the wind. It was no use. He was too tired and too sleepy. *He would just take a short nap, then be on his way again.*

Donagon drifted off and fell into a deep sleep. He dreamed about Jenny, and how it would be when they found each other. He had not understood his obsession with finding the girl until now. As he lay sleeping, he dreamed of a wedding day with Jenny standing by his side.

They were back on the farm at San Saba. Behind them with German steins raised high in salute were

Fuller and O'Hare. For the first time in the years of searching for Jenny, he knew why he could not give up on finding her. For the first time he knew he was in love with her. Now it was too late. He was going to die in a cold winter storm.

—————— ..... ——————

The crackling sound of a fire woke him and he lay still wondering if he were in heaven. For a long time he lay with his eyes closed. A sudden warmth came over him and he wondered how he could be so warm lying in a snow bank.

Dozing back off, he slept again. When he woke again, Donagon was sure he felt the heat of a warm fire. This time he opened his eyes and tried to look around. He was in a dark place. The only light was a low flame burning next to where he lay. When he turned, he saw the opening to a cavern close by. Hanging over the fire was a large blue porcelain pot and he smelled strong coffee brewing. *How did I get here?* Someone had found him in the snow and brought him into this cave.

His body finally started to thaw and he was able to sit up and pour a cup. It was a welcome feeling of warmth going into his body. For another two days, he was in and out of sleep. He was still too cold and weak to try to leave the cave and he never saw whoever had brought him to the place and saved his life.

From outside he heard the low murmur of voices and soon someone stepped into the cavern opening. "He's in here!"

Another man came alongside the first.

"Donagon, you alright?"

When he looked closer, he realized it was Fred Fuller standing there.

"Where did you come from?"

"Saw that big storm come up. Thought you might need help."

"Reckon I did. How did you get me in here?"

"We didn't We just saw a glow from that fire and come to see who was here." O'Hare spoke up.

"Well, how did I get in here, then?"

"Don't know. We saw your horse outside, and then saw the fire. Didn't see nobody around. Figured you found this cave."

"I don't even remember getting here. Last I knew I went to sleep where I fell in a drift."

"Well, snow bout stopped. You ready to get down off this mountain?"

"Fred, I'm about like you. I never want to see snow again. Let's get out of here!"

Fuller and O'Hare helped him make it through the snow and mounted on his horse.

"Somebody been feeding your horse too."

All of them scanned the surroundings and saw no one. The storm had stopped and the sky was bright blue and clear as they rode away from the cave. They did not see the lone figure watching from in the trees between the cabin and cave. Jenny Steinke made her way back into the cavern wondering who the men were and why they went back the same way they had come. She had not recognized the boy she once knew who was now a man.

Coming down to the flat land near the border, the three riders shed the heavy robes they had worn in the higher elevations.

"I reckon we can go around them mountains out toward El Paso."

"I reckon we can. I'm ready to get back to San Saba."

They followed the Rio Grande, and found their way across the south plain and then turned east. The trail led to the Pecos River. A week later when they crossed the Pecos, the wind began to blow and for the first time since they left the mountains, a storm was brewing. Snow began to fall in flurries at first, and then it became a full-blown blizzard. Fred Fuller was becoming nervous when the snow blew across their trail.

The weather in this part of Texas was unpredictable and one minute it could snow and the next a scorching desert wind would come up. This time it was to be a blizzard of great proportion. Snowdrifts were piling along both side of the trail as they headed east from the Pecos. Late in the day, they stopped to find cover and a place to build a fire for coffee. Twin boulders rose out of the landscape and through the blinding snow a fire was twinkling through the haze. Shouting above the wind, Donagon yelled at the camp.

"Hello, the camp. We're coming in!"

"Come ahead!" A head stuck out from under a poncho. "Best keep yore hands where I can see em."

The three riders rode in slow with their hands held high.

"What ya'll doing out there in that snow storm?"

"Trying to ride through it." Fred shook the snow from his poncho. "That coffee I smell?"

"Shore is. Help yoreself. Name is Hester T. Rollup. My Ma wanted a girl, I reckon. Where you boys headed?"

"Over on the San Saba. Where you going?"

"Headed fer them Big Bend mountains. Got a late start. Reckon it'll be hard to find a empty cabin by now."

"We saw one a couple of weeks ago. Close by a cave. Never can see anybody there. Second or third time we passed that way." Donagon shared their times at the cave.

"Know about that one. Some say it's haunted. Men been known to see a ghost woman running through them creeks and rivers round that place.

"We never saw anybody. Felt like somebody was always watching us though."

"That was probably that ghost woman they talk about."

"Don't believe in ghost." Donagon was still wondering who had pulled him into the cave.

The wind and snow kept up for another two days. The three searchers sat with the old man huddled around the fire and drinking hot coffee to keep warm. Finally, on the third day, the snow stopped and the wind slowed to a low breeze.

"Reckon I better get going fore it comes another storm. Need to get on up in them mountains fore winter sets in."

"What do you do in the mountains besides freeze?" Fred Fuller asked.

Trap them beaver. Ain't you never seen nobody trappin up there?"

"Guess not."

"Lots of money in them beaver pelts. If them Injuns don't steal em or you don't get shot."

"Good luck, Hester. I reckon we better get going too. Still two weeks to the San Saba."

"San Saba? Heard them Comanch been raiding over there again. Best watch out for your scalp." He waived and rode off pulling his packhorse behind him.

It did take them another two weeks to reach the river and two more days to ride within sight of the farm. The first thing they noticed was fields overgrown. It was not the Schroeder's to let that happen. They rode in slow, looking for signs of anyone about. O'Hare was the first one to spot it. He pulled rein and pointed to the large double doors of the barn. Ten or more arrows were stuck into the doors. There had been another raid on the farm. Riding around the barn and house, Fred was the first to see two more fresh piles of dirt with crosses at one end.

Chapter 14

Otherwise, the avenger of blood might pursue the
manslayer in the heat of his anger, and, overtake him, because
the way is long, and take his life, though he was not deserving of
death, since he had not hated him previously.
Deuteronomy 19:6

It had been nine years now since Jenny was taken
by the Comanche. Donagon had tried hard to hold
onto the farm for her return. With the help of Fred
Fuller he had managed to keep it up and going for all
these years. It was time to give it up. The two friends
looked at each other, then at O'Hare.

Fuller was the first to speak it aloud.

"Well, Irish, ever thought about being a Texas Ranger?"

"A what?"

"A Texas Ranger! I reckon we better get on to Austin." Donagon kicked his horse up and galloped down the river. Fuller was right behind him.

"Hey! Wait for me!" O'Hare rode after them. O'Hare had heard of the rangers, but had never thought about being one. He remembered fighting a battle with them when he was with the Comanche.

A week later, the three men rode up to the ranger headquarters in Austin and dismounted. Donagon and Fuller still remembered the place from years before. Climbing the steps, they strode into the office and saw a man seated at a desk in the long wide hallway.

"Who's in charge these days?" Donagon asked.

"Captain C. W. McWhorter. Who wants to know?"

"I'm Donagon. This is Fred Fuller and Juan O'Hare. We want to join the rangers."

"Ever been a ranger before?"

"Me and Fuller was once. Long time ago."

"Well, sign yore names. Sarge will give you a badge, if he got any left. Go through that door yonder." He pointed to the same door that Donagon had gone in years earlier.

The three of them walked down the hall and Fuller rapped on the door.

"Come!" A loud booming voice rang out.

They all walked into the large room with sunlight filtering through a burlap sack hanging from the window.

"Ya'll looking to be rangers?"

"Yep, that's what we're here for, Sarge."

124

"You got names?"

"I'm Donagon. This is Fred Fuller and Juan O'Hare."

"Raise your hands!" When they did, he spoke loud. "You solemnly swear to uphold the laws of the state of Texas?"

"I do!" They spoke in unison.

"Put your hands down. You're rangers now. Here's your badge! Get ready to go fight them Injuns. We leaving tomorrow morning early.

"Going after Comanche, Sarge?"

"Yep! Going down yonder to Corpus Christi. Ever been there?"

"Me and Fuller never been there. Don't know about O"Hare?"

"I been there."

"Good! You know how hot it is then. Captain wants us to patrol that area from Corpus Christi over to Goliad. Been some raids down there. Don't know for sure who's doing it. Some say Apache, some say Caddo or Tonkawa. I think it's Comanche. Reckon we'll find out. Best get some sleep. It's going to be a long ride."

"We'll be ready, Sarge. Sarge, you got a name?"

"I am Sergeant Wilcox, Franklin Wilcox, but you just call me Sarge."

_____ ….. _____

They and fifteen other rangers rode out at first light and headed south toward the coast of Texas. It would be their job to route all the Indians giving trouble and run them off or shoot them down. Another sergeant named Forest W. Gallwood took half of the rangers and turned toward Goliad, while Wilcox took Donagon, Fuller, O'Hare, and three others to Corpus Christi. Like the Sarge said, it was a long, hot ride.

Once they were on the outskirts of the coastal town, they had a run in with a small band of war painted Caddo's. The Indians did not stand and fight, but ran as soon as the rangers started firing at them.

Donagon thought about Jenny and wondered if they might find her in one of the Comanche parties. He was surprised the Comanche were this far south and near the coast. Most of what he heard was that they were in a war with Mexico and were hit and run on both sides of the border. When they were in Presidio, they saw signs of vicious attacks on Mexican ranches by Comanche.

When they arrived in Corpus Christi, they found that a Comanche war party had attacked a ranch on the west side of the community and ran off a bunch of cattle. They had shot and killed four ranch hands. There was a rumor that two whites wore the paint and rode with them. Some even said one of them was a woman, and that she had killed and scalped one of the cowhands.

Fuller and Donagon looked at one another when they heard it. Both riders hung back until the others were out of earshot.

"What do you think, partner?"

"Can't be Jenny. She wouldn't do that."

"Hard to say. She been gone nine years now. People do funny things, they been held captive that

126

long. Heard tell of one called Cynthia Parker, didn't want to come back."

"Heard that!" Donagon kicked his horse and rode ahead.

For days, they tracked the war party with no luck. The Comanche were very good at hiding their trail. O'Hare had said nothing about where he thought they might be. He rode along with the others and watched as one of the rangers kept dismounting and looking for tracks.

"Okay Irish, you going to show the Sarge which way they went?" Fuller knew his friend knew where they had gone.

"I'm not the scout!"

"Whose side are you on?"

"I am not a Comanche!" He kicked his horse and rode ahead of the rest.

Finally, after another three days, O'Hare approached the Sarge.

"Sarge, them Comanche ain't going this way."

"How do you know?"

"They turned west a day ago. Keep going this way, we'll be in Mexico before long."

"Why didn't you say so?"

"I just did!" O'Hare dismounted and knelt on the ground. "These tracks was made by Tonkawa. They don't ride horses. Comanche never walk anywhere."

"He's right Sarge" Donagon spoke up.

"Why didn't he say so before now?"

"He ain't the scout."

"He is now." Sergeant Wilcox glared at the other ranger who had been following the trail of a walking band of Tonkawa.

"Okay, O'Hare you go find em!"

Juan pulled rein, jerked his horses head around and galloped off. The others followed at a slower pace. For two days, the rangers followed the trail of Juan O'Hare across a desert floor, never catching sight of anything but his tracks. Late on the third day, silhouetted against a bright orange ball on the western horizon, a lone rider came into view. He sat tall in the saddle and waved at the rangers.

O'Hare waited until the others caught up.

"They're headed for the springs, Sarge."

"What springs?"

"Comanche springs. It's a watering hole for them Comanche when they raid into Mexico."

Donagon and Fuller exchanged glances. They both knew all about the springs.

"How far?"

"Another day, but they won't be there."

"How do you know?"

"Cause they are headed back to the nations. They've finished their raid."

Sergeant Wilcox looked at O'Hare, then the others. "We'll make camp here." He jumped from his horse and walked off.

—————— ····· ——————

O'Hare was right. There were no Comanche at the springs. Nor anyone else. Sergeant Wilcox decided to rest the animals and the rangers for a couple of days and then reconnoiter.

There was no use in tracking the Indians back into the nations. They would just disappear into all the other Comanche who had stayed on the reservation.

"What now, Sarge?" Fuller asked.

"Reckon we'll go on back to Austin and get new orders."

"Mind if me and Donagon go on to the nations and see if we can find them white folks?"

"Donagon stopped unsaddling his horse when he heard Fuller. He was surprised at his request.

"Can't stop you."

Donagon turned to Fuller. "You do know it's winter up there?"

"Can't be no worse than them mountains."

"Well, I reckon I better go and look after you two yahoo's!" O'Hare quipped.

At first light three Rangers rode away from Comanche springs headed north.

"Reckon there's any truth about that woman taking scalps?" It was Fuller bringing it up again.

"Ain't never seen any Comanche brave would let a woman do that!" O'Hare spoke from his days with the Comanche.

It took them another ten days to find the Red river and cross over into the Oklahoma territory. Snow was beginning to fall and the open flatlands, was soon covered with a white blanket.

By November, the three rangers had covered half the tribes who were scattered across the nations. They stopped and spent three or four days in each village looking for any information about a white woman.

The Choctaw, Cherokee, Caddo, and Tonkawa were all friendly and tried to help them find what they were looking for. The Comanche did not offer anything. O'Hare tried to use his time with them to gather any word of the white woman, who had been taken by them, from the Steinke farm. There was nothing.

Finally, the rangers had covered all the villages of the Comanche and decided it was time to get back to Austin for another assignment. They crossed back over the Red River and headed south. It was a good feeling to be back in Texas.

Three days after they crossed the river, they rode into Fort Worth. A huge celebration was going on. Men were riding up and down the streets firing their six guns and shouting.

Donagon stopped one of the celebrators and asked. "What's going on?"

"Didn't you hear? Fort Worth is now a Texas city."

The three rangers looked at each other. After three months of riding across the Indian nation, all they wanted was a bath and a real bed. They rode through the partiers and found a hitching rail in front of a hotel Stepping up onto the boardwalk; they stopped and watched the celebration for a few minutes, then walked into the lobby. The front desk had a line formed half way across the room. The tired rangers took one look and decided it was too long to wait.

O'Hare walked to one side of the desk and whispered something in the clerk's ear. The desk clerk looked at him somewhat funny, then turned and removed a key from a peg and handed it to him. He turned and waved to Donagon and Fuller. They followed him up the stairs and he turned the key in a room lock and opened it into a suite.

"What did you tell that man?"

130

"I told him we was here to get a room for the governor. This is it."

"Did you tell him we wanted to take a bath while we was waiting for the governor?"

"Water be here any minute!"

A knock on the door turned them and two men entered with buckets of hot water and whisked past them into another room with a long tub.

Donagon caught one of them by the arm as he was leaving.

"Would you bring the governor's escort three big steaks with potatoes and a big pot of coffee?"

"Yes sir. Be right up!"

When the tub was filled they each took a hot bath and then enjoyed a steak dinner on the governor. Just as they were dozing off a knock woke them.

A man with a black suit and tall hat stood in the doorway.

"The governor is here. He's ready for his room now."

Chapter 15

As often as the trumpet sounds, he says, "Aha!" And he
scents the battle from afar, And the thunder of the captains and
the war cry. Job 39:25

"Thought that was you boys. I had to near bout
beat it out of that clerk who you said you was. Heater
T. Rollup, boys. Remember me. We met out yonder
on the trail. Ya'll still lookin for that white young
un?"

"Yes, we are. Have you seen her?" Donagon's interest peaked.

"Heard tell where she was. Don't know she still there. Member me telling you I was gonna find that empty cabin?"

"You mean up in the Big Bend?"

"That's the one. Went up there lookin fer that cabin and guess what I found?"

"What?"

"An empty cabin!"

"Well, what about the girl. You said you knew something about the girl!"

"Oh, that. Met a feller said he seen a white woman traipsing about up in them mountains."

"Who? What fellow?" Donagon was getting aggravated with the old man.

"Name of Whiskey Dan. Drinks a lot!"

"Where is this Whiskey Dan?"

"I reckon he's still in them mountains. I left early. Weren't no beaver to be found?"

"Where is he in the mountains?"

"Last time I seen him, he was running off up to that cabin mumbling to hisself!"

"Can you take us to it?"

"Shore, come next winter. Don't care fer them mountains in the summer. Too many varmints around. Ya'll got anything to drink?"

Donagon looked at the other two. His urge was to saddle up and ride back to the Big Bend Mountains. It was the first time in years; someone had said they saw Jenny.

"Wait a minute, Donagon. You going to believe a drunk old geezer like that?" Fuller asked.

"It's the first time anybody said they saw her."

"No. He said somebody else said they saw a white woman. Somebody called Whiskey Dan?"

"It's the only clue I have. I've got to go see for myself."

"You don't even know where to look." O'Hare spoke up.

"What about that cave you found me in. Somebody had to put me in there!"

"Don't mean it was her. You didn't see nobody!"

"Just the same. I have to go see. You coming?"

"I reckon. We done been all over the nations ten times. Might as well go back to them mountains. Least it won't be cold."

———————— ….. ————————

After a good night's sleep and a hot bath and shave, they headed south one more time in search of a ghost. In the nearly ten years of looking, no one had ever said he had actually seen Jenny. Donagon had never given up the search, and felt he was getting close to finding her. He had never spoke to his two friends about the way he felt for Jenny in his heart.

Heading west from Fort Worth, their first stop was in Abilene. Abilene was a busy town. Small, but the saloon there was wide open with gambling and other things.

It was already dark by the time the three riders rode under the street lanterns on the main street. Finding a hotel, they first took their ponies to a livery stable down the street. Walking down the boardwalk, they encountered four men who did not want to give way and let them pass.

"Donagon?"

Donagon turned to look at the voice calling his name.

"Ben Walters. We met out on the trail long time ago. You ever find that girl you was lookin for?"

"Hi, Ben." Donagon was searching through his brain for a name and face. "No, we ain't found her yet."

He had met so many men in his search for Jenny. All their names and faces were running together.

"I heard she was sold to a trapper Donagon. If that helps any?"

"Thanks Ben." Donagon was still unsure of the face. They passed and walked on down the street.

Sitting in the hotel café drinking coffee the next morning, Donagon, Fuller, and O'Hare saw the man called Ben Walters walking across the street. Donagon suddenly remembered who he was and where he had seen him before. Without a word to the others, he jumped to his feet and ran out the door.

"Ben! Ben Walters!"

The man turned. "Hello, Donagon."

"Sorry about last night. It's been a while. What did you say about Jenny?"

"Who?"

"Jenny. The girl I am looking for. You said something about a trapper?"

"Oh yeh. She was bought from them Comanch by a trapper. Don't recall his name. Seems he was headed up into them Big Bend Mountains with her. Winters get long up there you know."

It must have been Jenny! His mind raced to the cave someone had dragged him into. *But why didn't she know it was he?*

"Thanks, Ben." He wheeled and walked hurriedly back to where he had left his two friends.

"It was Jenny who dragged me into that cave!"

"How do you know that? You didn't remember anything."

"I just know. It had to be her. I'm ready to ride."

"Mind if we finish our coffee?" O'Hare quipped.

—————- ….. —————

They left Abilene with Donagon out in front of the other two. He had a goal and a place to go look for Jenny now. He was sure he would find her in a cave in the mountains. It had been ten long years and a long trail and he was ready for it to end.

Gunfire abruptly brought him back to the moment. He whirled in the saddle to see O'Hare topple from his horse. Fuller was turning to return fire at a band of Indians who had come from out of nowhere. There was no cover, so Fuller dismounted and pulled his horse to the ground, using him for cover. Donagon began firing at the oncoming band. There was ten or twelve of them and all painted for war. They were Comanche.

Fuller caught a bullet in his right arm and dropped his rifle. Donagon fired again and a brave catapulted from his mount. Six of the warriors surrounded Fuller and Donagon saw no use in keeping up the fight. He stood and raised his arms into the air. Fuller did the same. Both of them were knocked to the ground with the blunt end of a tomahawk.

Donagon vaguely remembered being thrown over the back of a horse and felt his hands being tied, before he lost consciousness. When he woke, it was pitch black and all he could see was the low glimmer of a flame some fifty feet away. He heard a groan, and tried to see who had made the sound. It was too dark to see.

"Fuller?" he whispered.

"Yeh, Donagon?"

"Yeh. What about O'Hare?"

"I think they got him back there."

"I thought all these Comanche were in the nations."

"Guess not. At least these ain't."

"Wonder what they going to do with us."

"Probably going to sell us to them silver miners. You remember them silver mines, don't you?"

"Yeh. We don't want to do that! Can you get your hands loose?"

"I been trying. Arm hurts some."

"We better keep trying."

Both men kept twisting and turning their wrist trying to loosen the rawhide straps. The Indians were asleep and had put no one to watch them. Just before daylight, they were getting desperate to get away and were pulling with all their might against the bonds.

Donagon felt his hands suddenly fall free from the rawhide. A voice whispered softly to him. "Don't move yet."

Fuller's hand dropped too.

"Okay, let's crawl out of here before them redskins wake up."

"O'Hare?"

"There's an arroyo fifty yards over yonder. We better get there fast."

Donagon and Fuller followed on their bellies as O'Hare crawled away. They stopped every couple of minutes to look at the fire. It took them about ten minutes to fall into the wash and roll to the bottom. The sun was peeking over the horizon as they started following the winding crevice away from their captors.

They were on foot, and the Comanche were horseback and it would not be hard for them to get caught. Running and stumbling, they kept following the arroyo as fast as they could. Fuller's arm was throbbing with pain from the gunshot wound.

None of them had a weapon, except for O'Hare's knife and six-gun. The Comanche had left him for dead and had not taken his weapons. He took the rear so he could cover their backs. For an hour, they moved as fast as they could, and then stopped for a breather.

Gasping, Fuller spoke through his pain. "I don't think they're coming."

"They don't have to. They know we're going to die out here anyway. No horses, no water, no food."

"We still got our feet."

"Let me look at your arm." Donagon reached for Fuller's bloody shirt.

"It's just a flesh wound. It'll be alright."

"I'll find a cactus pear and make a poultice." O'Hare fell back on his Comanche upbringing.

"We better keep moving." Fuller walked away.

The arroyo went on for another half mile and then ended on a flat desert terrain.

"Which way you think we ought to go?" Fuller asked.

"West! Comanche springs can't be more than three or four days from here."Donagon was sure about where they were.

"If them Comanche ain't there?" O'Hare said.

They found an abundance of prickly pear cactus and were able to get to the sweet, pulpy fruit with the knife O'Hare salvaged. That was their only source of water. By the end of the first day, the sun had taken a toll on all three of them. They decided to walk on through the night while the sun was down.

At first light, they found a small cluster of mesquite trees and curled up as close as they could for some semblance of shade. They were exhausted and all three slept until the sun was disappearing in the west. Eating their fill of the sweet fruit, they began another trek through the dark desert air. They had seen no sign of the Comanche.

Before they found a place to sleep out of the sun, O'Hare managed to shoot a jackrabbit with one shot from his six-gun. They built a fire with mesquite sticks and had their first meal in three days. It was slow moving at night, not knowing what lay in front of them. There was no moon out to help light the way and they spent much of the night stumbling along, tripping over rocks and unseen cactus.

By daylight on the fourth day, they were getting close to the springs They slowed their pace and strained to see if there was any signs of the Comanche. It appeared that there was no one anywhere near the bubbling water springs.

They crept on their hands and knees until they were close enough to be sure they were alone. When they had decided that, they got up and ran to the edge of the cool, clear pond. The three rangers fell face first into the pool of pure, clean water. Covering their heads, they drank their fill and then splashed the cold liquid all over their parched and burning bodies.

After they had satisfied their thirst, they all found shade under the trees on the edge of the springs and slept the day through.

Fuller was the first to wake, then Donagon.

"How's your arm?"

"It's good. Don't hurt much now. Guess that poultice O'Hare put on there, helped."

"I told you it would." O'Hare rolled over and sat up.

"Anybody got any idea where we go from here?"

"Well, I see two choices. Either we go back where we come from and try to find some horses, or we keep walking south to the Rio Grande. That'll put us close to them mountains, but I don't like walking up there."

Chapter 16

And He did not let him, but He said to him, "Go home to
your people and report to them great things the Lord has done for
you, and how he had mercy on you. Mark 5:19

She watched as two men went into the cave and
found the man she had dragged in there. They had not
seen her observing from in the trees. There had been
something familiar about the man, but it could not
have been anybody she had known. Every man who
had been in her life was dead.

She turned and walked back to the cabin she had called home for almost ten years. For the first time in all her years on the mountain, Jenny felt a yearning to be with other people of her kind. There was no way to describe the feeling that was coming over her.

Sitting in the cabin, she felt a chill in her bones and could not figure out what was bothering her. Jenny Steinke could not sit still and let this feeling overcome her. She wrapped herself in a doeskin robe and walked out into the cold, blowing beginning of a snowstorm.

First, she went to the cave and sat looking through the wide entrance at the falling snow, then back out into the cold. Something about being in the cave she had never felt before. Something about the man, she had helped. *Maybe he was supposed to be the one to replace the only love she had ever known. But! How could she find him now?*

Walking until the snow was getting deep around her, she went back to the cabin and sat staring at the fire. After a while, she fell asleep and slept through the night in the warmth of the dying embers. She woke early and felt a hunger that she had not felt in a long time. She removed some of the smoked fish from her smoke house and indulged herself.

———————— ..... ————————

A large figure of a man moved slowly through the falling snow. He was dressed in buckskins and a coonskin cap pulled down to cover his ears. His beard was long and scraggly, cascading in a dirty cluster down his chest. Most of his teeth had been lost through years of chewing tobacco and drinking rotgut whiskey. One of his eyes was clouded over by a white film from a fight he'd had with one of his fellow trappers.

Whiskey Dan was not sure, if he had really seen what he thought he had, or if it was a figment of his imagination. He thought he had seen a white woman flitting through the trees, near a cabin and then she would disappear into the ground somewhere. This time he was determined to see if she was real.

He crept slowly through the trees staying low. Every few minutes he stopped to scan the horizon, looking for a movement. When he had circled around the cabin, he found a place to sit and watch. This time he meant to see where she disappeared. Through the haze, he could see a slim, narrow wisp of smoke rising from the cabin chimney. Sitting on a tree stump, he waited.

It was near dark when the cabin door opened and a shadowy ghost of a figure slipped out and walked slowly through the trees. This time Whiskey Dan was there to see where she went. He sat still and watched as she stopped and looked around, then as before, just dropped out of sight. This time he knew the spot.

Waiting for a minute to see that she did not reappear, he slinked forward to where she had gone. When he got to the spot, he looked around and saw only small footprints leading to a dark spot in a large boulder. *How could she have just left?*

Cautiously, he stole forward until he finally saw it. There was an opening to some sort of cavern. Easing forward, he slid inside the opening until he was standing in a large room. In another room some twenty feet away, he saw the glow of a small fire. Sliding against one wall of the cave, he eased along until he could see into the smaller room.

It looked as if someone had spent many days or years creating a cabin like atmosphere in the cavern back room. It was totally out of sight from the outside world. He took one more step and his shadow fell across the low flame and moved across the face of a small person sitting there. She turned and reached for a long knife, lying at her side.

Whiskey Dan made a lunging motion toward the small figure and felt the sting of a sharp blade as it penetrated his fat stomach. Clawing at the air, he tried to grab onto the woman holding the knife. She let go and stepped back with both hands covering her mouth. Jenny Steinke had spent ten years on this mountain and had never had to hurt anyone. Now she had taken the life of another human being. Her mountain would no longer be the same.

She staggered out of the cave and made her way toward the cabin, stopping along the way to vomit everything from her body. For several minutes, she leaned against a tree and retched until there was nothing left. *What would she do now?*

Jenny made it into the cabin and wiped her face and eyes. She drank a long pull of water from a skin and then sank to her knees in front of the fireplace.

_____ ….. _____

144

She slumped on the floor and sought sleep but it was a long time coming. When she woke up it was daylight outside and the snow had stopped falling. The sky had cleared and turned a clear blue. Before she had found sleep, she had made up her mind what she must do.

She pulled on her deerskin knee high boots that she had fashioned from the hide of a buck she had killed with a bow. Next was a robe that she had made the same way. A hat she had made from the skin of a beaver went on her head.

Taking one last look around, she slung a water skin over her shoulder and a knife in her waistband. For the first time in ten years, Jenny Steinke was ready to return to the outside world. She had no idea where she was going or how she would get there. All she knew was to retrace the trail she had taken many years before to get to this place. That would lead her back down the mountain.

She started out slowly and watched the animals and birds as they prepared for another spring. She saw beaver playing in the streams as the snow was slowly beginning to melt away.

At night, she found shelter under or near rocks or boulders. She had packed a supply of venison jerky, so she was not hungry. She was in no hurry to rejoin her old world. Her last encounter with people was as a twelve-year old girl.

Once she had seen an Apache brave sitting astride a horse on a peak far away. He did not see her. A large brown bear had slinked past her hiding place in the rocks. She was still in her world with all the birds and animals around her. It frightened her to think what she would find, when she were exposed to people.

145

After several days of descending the mountain, she came to the place where the trapper who had bought her was still lying. At least his bones and the arrows in his back marked his resting place. She skirted around the bones and continued down the trail.

For more than a week, Jenny flirted with her friends along the trail. Finally, she was finding herself in the foothills of the Big Bend Mountains. The air had gotten warmer and soon she was on the bank of the Rio Grande River. She removed her boots and sat on the bank, dangling her feet in the cool, clear, water.

She had no idea which way to go, so decided that downstream would make more sense. Pulling her boots back on she struck out, following the river to wherever it led her.

_____ ..... _____

The weather began to heat up as she followed the riverbank. She was beginning to yearn for something to eat besides the jerky she had brought with her. Walking along the river, she saw fish swimming along the bank.

Jenny fashioned a fishing trap from short mesquite limbs. She dropped it into the river, then watched and waited, building a small fire. It wasn't long before she had trapped a trout and scraped it clean and put it over the fire. She was unaware of someone watching her from across the river.

She enjoyed her first meal in days and topped it off with a drink of fresh cold water from the river. While she was raising the water to her mouth, she was gazing across the river at two red men standing and watching her. She jumped to her feet and pulled the knife from her waist.

One of the Indians raised one hand in greeting. "We no fight. We are Tonkawa. We are friends. Come, we show you."

Jenny was not sure of what to do. She knew she could not win in a battle with the two big red men, so she followed them. They walked on the Mexico bank and she stayed on her side. For four hours, she followed along, watching for others to join the Indians.

Suddenly, she saw in front of her, on her side of the river, a circle of teepees rising out of the landscape. There were women and children walking all about. The women tended cook fires and the children were laughing and playing some kind of game with a hoop.

The two she had followed stepped into the river and waded across. For the first time since she had fallen in behind them, they turned and waved to her. There was nothing else for her to do, but walk into the village.

Surprising to her, all the Indians she saw were smiling and waving to her in a friendly way. It was her first encounter with so many people in ten years. Jenny was relieved to find so many smiles. She was quickly surrounded, by children, and felt welcomed by all the others. One of the women led her to a place by a fire and motioned her to sit.

Some of the others began bringing her food and water. A tall man came from inside the teepee in front of her.

"I am Brown beaver. I am chief of this band. Welcome to my village."

"I am Jenny Steinke. Thank you for your kindness." Her own voice sounded funny to her.

"What you do out here alone, Jenny Steinke?"

"I am on my way home. I have been in the Big Mountain for many years. Now it is time to go back to my people."

"Where Jenny people?"

"I am not sure. I think I will go to the San Saba River."

"We will go with you, Jenny Steinke. Tomorrow, we go with you. Today, we celebrate you come to us. Bring more food! Sing, dance!"

The Tonkawa were a very nice and friendly people and Jenny felt at ease to be with them. She was glad that her first meeting with people was with them. They were a happy people and the celebration went on the rest of the day and long into the night. Finally, one of the women showed her to a teepee so she could sleep.

_____ ..... _____

At first light, the women were back at their cook fires preparing food for their men and children. As soon as all of them had eaten, they began to break camp. It was a smooth thing to watch as the women broke down the teepees and loaded them on travois pulled by dogs.

By mid-morning, a caravan was moving across the south Texas desert headed north. Jenny fell in with them and played with the children as she walked. It would be a long, hot journey to their destination.

Jenny thought about the man from whom she had taken a life. It brought back a flood of other memories. She wondered about the man she had dragged into the cave, only to see him taken by two other men. She thought about her parents and recalled the vision of them, scalped by the Comanche. Remembering, her time as a hostage, she saw in her mind, the death of the only man she had ever felt love.

Trying to clear her mind from all those thoughts, she began talking to some of the Tonkawa women, and asking about their life. She found that this was to be their last move as a free people. They were going on to the Indian Nations and move on to a reservation.

Chapter 17

Beloved, let us love one another, for love is from God; and everyone who loves, is born of God and knows God.
1 John 4:7

The three rangers were still at Comanche springs with no horses to ride out of there.

"I think we ought to go back somewhere and find us a horse. I don't think it would be smart to walk all the way to Big Bend."

"I think you're right Fuller. Maybe we can steal ours back from them Comanche."

Donagon listened to his two partners. He knew they were right, but he still felt the need to go find Jenny. He wanted to move on to the mountains, but decided to go along with their plan. It would not be easy to find the Comanche. He had trailed and tracked them for years without getting close to them very often.

When they had gotten their fill of the cool water, they began a trek to the north. Oneida was probably two weeks or more of walking, but there was a post office at the Yellow house draw about halfway. Maybe they could find horses there.

After the first three days, they were running low on water and getting blisters on their feet. The soles of their boots were beginning to wear thin. Donagon did not want to stop and rest when the others did, so he managed to separate from them by several hundred yards.

He continued to gain distance on them as the days progressed, and by the sixth day, he was no longer in sight. He was down to eating prickly pear cactus for water. Without the knife that O'Hare was carrying, he had to get to the pulp with his fingers. The thorns were making sores on his fingers.

By late afternoon, he saw a yellow painted building in the distance. Tied out front were seven or eight horses. His attitude improved, knowing that they could now find a way to get three of the animals from the owners. He took longer steps to increase his pace and get to the yellow building before they left. He was within two hundred yards when four men backed out the door, one carrying a postal bag over his shoulder. Gunfire erupted as one of the men fired into the building. Donagon ducked behind a boulder, and watched the four saddle up and ride off. One of them

151

was holding on to a wounded left shoulder. When they were gone, he made his way on to the yellow building. As he stepped inside, a man in the shadows pointed a gun in his direction.

"Don't move mister."

"Hold on. I'm not armed! I saw them four rob you and ride off."

"Where did you come from?"

"I'm afoot. I been walking for a week from Comanche springs. Comanche got my horse and two others with me."

"Where's them others, then?"

"They'll be along. What happened here?"

"Got payroll money for the mine over in Yellow house draw. Them varmints musta found out about it. Weren't nobody supposed to know but the foreman and me."

"Who's them other horses belong to?"

"Two of em belong to them two dead ones over there in the corner. Tried to stop them owlhoots. One is mine."

'Well, me and my partners are Texas Rangers. When they get here, we'll go after them outlaws."

"Got another horse?"

"We'll use those three out there."

"One of them is mine. You can't take my horse!"

"Can, and will! It's official Texas Ranger business."

"Hold on now, mister. You ain't got a gun and I do. How you going to take my horse?"

"By me pointing my gun at you."

O'Hare walked in from the bright sunlight.

"Hold on now. You supposed to be rangers. Rangers don't steal horses."

"We ain't stealing your horse, mister. We are borrowing it to chase them robbers."

"What robbers?" Fuller looked at Donagon.

"You hadn't been so slow, you would have seen them four outlaws rob this post office and ride off. They shot them two men yonder." He pointed to the two bodies in the corner.

"Well, we better ride after them." Fuller said.

"I'll bring your horse back when we get that payroll back."

"How am I supposed to get home? It's four miles to my cabin!"

"Walk, I reckon, like we did."

———— ….. ————

The three rangers mounted the three horses and rode out after the four who had done the payroll robbery. The tracks were easy to follow on the dry sandy ground. They rode North, and probably headed for Oneida. The rangers fell in behind the tracks and followed along at a slow pace. If they didn't catch them before, it would be easy to find them in the town.

On the second day, they had caught up with the outlaws and could see the dust from their trail in the distance. Kicking their horses up, they rode at a gallop until they were in sight of the four riders.

One of them had looked back and seen the rangers coming, and the four kicked their mounts and the race was on. None of the horses was fresh, so one could outdistance the other. Slowly the rangers began to gain on the outlaws. When they were within a hundred yards, one of the four fired a volley of shots at the rangers. The only one capable of shooting back was O'Hare. He fired and one of the outlaws tumbled from his horse.

Donagon stopped where the man had fallen and took his weapon from its holster. He also removed a rifle from the boot. Catching back up with Fuller, and O'Hare, he fired a shot from the rifle and dropped another one. The other two, one was already wounded, pulled rein and held their hands up.

The rangers surrounded them and held them at gunpoint. Fuller dismounted and retrieved their long guns and took their pistols. The one who was wounded, held up the postal bag and O'Hare took it from him. Donagon tied their hands behind them, and they all turned and headed back toward the Yellow post office. It was late in the day so after an hour they stopped and made camp.

Three days later, they rode back up to the yellow post office and dismounted. The postmaster was not there, and the building locked. Since Donagon had taken his horse, he would not walk the four miles to work.

Donagon mounted up and rode to the postmaster's home, leading the horse behind one of the outlaw horses. He wanted to get back on the trail to finding Jenny.

"What you gonna do with them two?" The postmaster asked.

"What do you mean?"

"We ain't got no jail!"

"You got a bag full of money and a working mine, build one!"

"Now see here! You are Texas rangers, you supposed to take care of them."

"They didn't rob us. You want us to give them the money back and turn them loose. We hadn't just showed up here you wouldn't have your money back."

"Well, I reckon the mine owner will take care of them."

"I reckon they will."

———————— ….. ————————

The first thing the following morning, the rangers rode out on horses they had confiscated from the dead outlaws. Donagon was anxious to get back on the trail. He knew that this time he was going to find Jenny in a cabin or a cave in Big Bend. They rode long days because he wanted to go as far as they could every day.

It felt good to the Rangers to be back in the saddle and have side arms and rifles again. If the Comanche struck again, they would be ready for them.

"You really think we are going to find her this time? We have followed good leads before you know."

"I know, but this time I just feel it. That trapper was sure it was her, that was seen.

155

"We'll see."

Donagon spurred his horses and rode off. It seemed the faster they rode, the longer it was taking to get to the springs. He slowed and dropped back with the other two.

"If we don't find her this time, we'll go back to rangering and forget about it."

"I think you're right. We been looking for ten years now. If we haven't found her by now, don't reckon we are going to."

For five more days, they rode pretty much in silence, each with their own thoughts. On the morning of the sixth day, they spotted the Comanche springs on the horizon and expected they would be there by days end.

As they rode close to the springs, Fuller looked up and pointed to the south.

"Indians. They're on foot. Don't look like Comanche."

They're not Comanche." O'Hare said. "I think they are Tonkawa. Tonkawa don't ride horses. They are still a day off. I reckon we'll know by tomorrow.

Donagon built a fire and put on a pot of coffee while Fuller started a pan of fatback and flat bread.

"What would you do if you weren't a ranger?" O'Hare asked the other two.

"Don't know. I reckon I would be a sheriff in a small town somewhere." Fuller's answered.

"I think I would go back to being a farmer. Steinke farm is still there. It's kinda like home. Lots of good memories there."

"I thought you didn't like farming?"

"I didn't, but it puts me in mind of Jenny. I think it's what she would want to do. Like her Ma and Pa."

"Just can't picture you being a farmer."

"I can." Fuller spoke up. "I farmed with Donagon a few years. I think it's in his blood."

"I reckon I'm going to get some sleep. I guess Donagons going to want to leave at first light. He's in a big hurry to get to them mountains."

"I reckon."

It was just getting dark good when the three of them rolled up in a bedroll. Donagon had a restless, fitful night, thinking about what he would find down the trail. If he found Jenny, he would give up being a ranger and go back to farming. He fell asleep with that thought.

At sunrise, the band of Indians started coming into the springs and setting up their teepees. They were a fair size village and the women were all busy setting up the camp when the rangers were rolling out of their beds. They had fires going and the smell of food was already permeating the air.

Brown beaver had recognized the rangers from their earlier meeting. He invited them to come and talk. Donagon remembered that time when the Tonkawa braves talked all day and halfway through the night. He was anxious to get back on the trail.

The three rangers had not seen the white woman that was traveling with the Tonkawa. She was busy helping the other women set up their teepees.

Fuller and O'Hare were saddling their horses, while Donagon was gone to the pond to fill the blue porcelain coffee pot.

When they turned to go start their fire, they were startled to see a young white woman among the Tonkawa. They watched as she worked with the others. They looked to see where Donagon was and if he had seen her. He was on the edge of the pond, dipping the coffee pot.

The white woman picked up a vessel and walked toward the pond where Donagon was bending to fill the coffee pot.

They weren't sure of who the woman was, but they had a suspicion. They watched as she approached beside him and squatted down next to him to fill the water vessel. Donagon turned to see who had stopped beside him, and his friends watched as the blue porcelain pot fell from his hands into the pond.

While they watched, Donagon rose slowly to his feet. He stared intently at the young woman for a minute. Finally, he managed to choke words out of his mouth.

"Jenny, is that you?"

"Who are you?"

"I am David, Jenny. David Donagon."

"David is dead. I saw him die."

"I am not dead, Jenny. I have searched for you for all these years."

She looked deep into the eyes of the man before her.

'What was my parent's names? Where did we live?"

"Your father was John. Your mother was Mary. She taught you and me how to make biscuits! We lived on a farm on the San Saba River. It is me, Jenny! It is David."

Fuller and O'Hare watched their friend speaking to the young white woman. They couldn't hear what he was saying, but by his look, they knew who the girl was.

Jenny stared deeper into his eyes. "David. Is it really you?"

Suddenly, the two friends saw a man and woman fall into each other's arms. They knew that the hunt for Jenny Steinke was over.

For this and other titles by Francis Louis Guy Smith, please go to www.booksbyguy.com or Kindle All titles are also available at Amazon books.

Winds of Freedom
Winds of the Rio Grande
Santa Fe Sundown
Winds of Ah-Mah-Ree-yuh
Tonkawa
Cain
Matilda
Pascal vol.1
Pascal vol. 2
Sinclair
The Salado Kid
Skeeter
Cocheta
McAllister vol.1
McAllister vol. 2
Peg
Harriman and Summers
Donagon
Winds of the Promised Land.
Oath of Color

Made in the USA
San Bernardino, CA
14 November 2014